WIRED DARK

Paradise Crime Book 4

TOBY NEAL

D0765130

WIRED DARK

A Paradise Crime Novel

TOBY NEAL

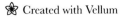

Get Two Books Free!

Visit
www.subscribepage.com/TobyNealNews

"Glam (style) really did plant seeds for a new identity. I think a lot of kids needed that sense of reinvention. Kids learned that however crazy you may think it is, there is a place for what you want to do and who you want to be."
    ~David Bowie

"In the social jungle of human existence, there is no feeling of being alive without a sense of identity."
    ~Erik Erikson

"We are all instinctively struggling to reach our potential —and some of us completely remake ourselves numerous times in order to do so."
    ~Toby Neal

Chapter One

H is wife's room was almost ready for her.

Assan Ang looked around a bare white space. He liked the simplicity of it: just a king-size bed, and the great wheel mounted on the wall with all its straps and accoutrements. Off to the side, a locked metal cabinet.

No windows. Windows were just an opportunity for escape and distraction, and he liked to keep her in the dark when he wasn't visiting.

The floor was covered with a deep, plush collection of hand-knotted Persian rugs. A screen hid a toilet, plastic shower stall, and sink in the corner. The door into the hallway was sound-proofed and reinforced. A slit in the bottom with a metal flap provided enough space for a plate to slide in so that he could feed her.

The king-size bed dominated the room. An iron bedstead, already equipped with restraints, was set off by white satin sheets. White looked good against Sophie's tawny skin, the rich golden-brown color of good tea with just a bit of cream in it. *He could hardly wait to see her naked on that bed.*

Assan walked over and unlocked the steel cabinet filled with instruments of pleasure and torture. Just looking at the floggers, dildos, rings, clamps, blades, and electrodes made him smile.

Breaking her again was going to be such a joy.

Doms in the lifestyle were supposed to find willing submissives to partner with. To his mind, that defeated the whole purpose.

Assan took their wedding photo out of his pocket and sat down on the bed, holding it in his hand. Spending time in memories of their marriage and rehearsing the excitement to come kept him focused—and he needed to stay focused. Sophie had proved harder to retrieve than he had ever anticipated.

Sophie's face seemed to glow in the photo. Her radiant smile, from within the frame of her wedding veil, was filled with a young woman's naïve hope. She had been a true beauty back then, with a face that could have decorated magazine covers, and a body to match.

Her recent mutilation enraged him. *She was his to destroy. No one else's.*

Assan's own visage in the photo was not as pleasant to look at, but in the picture his mouth was curved in a smile of happy anticipation. He distinctly remembered how he had felt that day: *flush with victory.*

He'd been delighted in the arranged marriage to Sophie Smithson, debutante daughter of an American diplomat and related to Thai royalty on her mother's side. His bride had been a catch for anyone: beautiful, intelligent, cultured, and sweet. He'd been hopeful, back then, that he could keep his dark preferences separate from his marriage. Hopeful that his business would continue to expand easily. Hopeful that Sophie was the biddable and easily impregnated young woman she appeared to be.

None of the things he'd hoped for had come true.

Rage surged through Assan. He restrained himself from crumpling the photo in his hand. Instead, he set it beside him on the expanse of satin, and smoothed its edges.

People didn't understand how much work went into setting up this kind of relationship. She'd been worth it once, and she would be again—*but she was never leaving this room alive.*

––––––

TECH SECURITY SPECIALIST Sophie Ang walked through the velvet-dark night, patrolling a beachfront property in Wailea on Maui. She found comfort in the familiar weight of her Glock on one hip as her hand rested on it, but she kept her arms loose, ready for action, as she scanned the area. Rocker Shank Miller's estate was as protected as Sophie and her Security Solutions partner, Jake Dunn, could make it—but something had set off one of the property's perimeter motion detectors, and it was Sophie's turn to check out the disturbance.

The hammered pewter gleam of moonlight reflected off a great swath of beach and rendered Miller's manicured lawn in shades of gray, casting ornamental plantings into black shadow. Natural stone pavers, set into the grass, made an easy route around the clustered ferns, flowering trees, and birds of paradise that ringed the grounds.

Jake had wanted to cut all the plantings way back to improve visibility and monitoring, but Miller had refused. "I didn't spend ten million on this getaway spot so I could hide out inside a cement bunker with no view," the rock star had said. "I come here to relax. Growing green stuff helps me relax, and so does my view. Do the best you can with those challenges, but I won't lose either."

Her partner never did anything by half measures, and he took Shank Miller's safety more seriously than the man did himself. Jake had supervised the installation of a Plexiglas wall to preserve that view, a bulletproof, impenetrable and almost invisible barrier on Sophie's left.

Sophie headed toward the corner closest to the beach where the alarm had sounded. Motion detectors, buried and almost invisible in the plantings, created frequent disturbances for their team, and Sophie was still getting used to being part of that team.

Jake took up a lot of personal space. Sometimes he made it hard for her to breathe, and it was that need for space that had driven Sophie to ask for a guest room inside the main house so that they weren't both occupying the small cottage that had become the team's security headquarters. The computer monitoring station had been moved from the main house out there too, and Jake stayed out there with their two backup operatives, Jesse Kanaka and Ronnie Fellowes.

Sophie reached the corner of the grounds where the alarm had gone off. Jake had wanted to put in lights that responded to the motion detectors, but Shank had put his boot-clad foot down again. "I can't have this place light up like a stadium every time a gecko runs across the freakin' fence."

That meant that the corner Sophie approached, hidden on the beach side by a clump of native bushes, was inky-dark. Sophie pulled out a powerful flashlight and shone it over the area. Illumination played over the smooth grass and shadowy foliage.

Nothing. Probably just a gecko, one of those ubiquitous Hawaiian lizards that hunted insects at night.

Sophie was moving on when the beam caught a flash of color. She turned and lit up the item.

Lying beneath a cluster of bird of paradise were a plastic bride and groom, the toys rubber-banded together, wrapped in each other's arms.

Sophie scanned for movement along the bushes of the public beach for any sign of who might have thrown the dolls into the compound, but the area was deserted.

Nothing to see but the gleam of the moon on the ocean, nothing to hear but the sound of the surf and the rustle of a gentle night wind in the palm trees overhead.

Sophie reached into her pocket and removed a small plastic

bag. She used it to pick up the figures, shining the light over a Barbie and Ken doll. The Barbie was dressed in a wedding gown, her long blonde hair braided, a veil over her face. The groom's molded plastic hair had been colored over with Sharpie, and squiggles of black ink trailed down inside the doll's tuxedo, representing Shank Miller's long dark locks—and the male doll's right hand, Miller's guitar hand, had been sawed off.

Chapter Two

Sophie loosened the bulletproof vest Jake had insisted they all wear since the plastic figures had begun appearing inside the compound, as she sat down with their team at the security cottage's small dining room table. Jake held the dolls in gloved hands, studying them. Per usual, there had been no prints on the dolls, now stripped to reveal detailed renditions of Shank Miller's tattoos drawn over the plastic of the "bridegroom."

"This situation is escalating." Jake's voice was grim.

Sophie looked up from securing her sidearm and met her partner's serious gunmetal-gray eyes. Illumination shone on Jake's buzz-cut dark hair, lighting up a big hard body dressed in all black combat clothing. Sophie couldn't remember the last time she'd seen the ex-Special Forces operative wear anything else. She nodded. "Looks like the unsub is increasing the symbolic aggression with each set of figures."

Shank Miller's stalking had begun months ago, triggering Miller to reach out to their private security company, seeking to prevent further incursions.

"It was kind of hard to take this seriously at first." Jesse

Kanaka, one of their young operatives, pointed to the figures. "But now Blondie is beginning to creep me out."

"I think that's her plan." Jake slipped the figures into the plastic evidence bag before they were submitted to Maui Police Department as part of the ongoing case. He sat back, rubbing the site of a recent gunshot wound on his shoulder. "The addition of the hand being cut off is not a good sign. I'm glad Shank told us he didn't want to know details. No sense his losing sleep over this, giving Blondie more bandwidth in his life than she's already taking up. So, let's review. What do we know?"

Sophie gazed around the table at their little team. Ronnie Fellowes was a criminal justice major at the University of Hawaii, and fresh out of the military. He had a deceptively naïve young face with the kind of forgettable, bland Caucasian features that Jake had told her were a positive attribute for security work. Ronnie took off a pair of wire-rimmed glasses and rubbed them on his sleeve. "So, you want to do a case review, boss?"

"Isn't that what I said?" Jake's voice was sharp with impatience—and something else—*anxiety.*

Sophie rarely ever saw any fear in Jake, and the vibration of his tone sharpened her attention. She sat up in her chair and leaned her elbows forward onto the table, turning to address Jesse. The Hawaiian-Filipino man was nervously scribbling on a yellow legal pad, his eyes down. Neither appeared confident enough to get the meeting started.

"When I was in the FBI and we were on a case at this stage, we often reviewed where we were on all of our leads. It's good investigative practice and can often jar loose new ideas. Jesse, would you mind using one of the markers to help us track everything on the whiteboard?"

Jesse stood with alacrity. Jake caught Sophie's eye for a moment and gave a tiny nod. She went on. "When did Shank Miller first become aware of Blondie?"

"Miller's publicist says that he began receiving love notes signed by Blondie along with underwear in the mail six months ago," Ronnie said.

"But she had likely been contacting him earlier than that," Jake said. "The publicist thinks she had been attending his concerts and events for years, throwing her panties at him whenever she got the chance—because she has some pretty distinctive panties."

Jesse, at the board, snorted a chuckle and drew a crude rendering of the white lace thongs trimmed with ivory ribbon that, along with the Barbie dolls, were the signature MO of their stalker. "She's got Shank Miller in mind for a wedding night."

"Don't underestimate the power of an obsessed fan, male or female," Sophie said sharply. "It's true that most deadly attacks are perpetrated by male fans, but Blondie has been getting more and more bold and aggressive toward Miller."

Jesse nodded, chastened, and erased the drawing.

Jake summarized. "Blondie seems to have begun as a typical fan, attending Shank's concerts and throwing her panties. While not a particularly savory practice, it's not uncommon for starstruck groupies to make these kinds of gestures. She went from that to sending Miller mail, along with continuing to attend the concerts and trying to reach him personally. When he began curtailing his appearances due to burnout, Blondie increased her attempts to interact by locating his home here on Maui and sending the dolls through the mail, all dressed in wedding clothes. All of this led to Miller realizing that he was more vulnerable than he knew, and he hired us to secure the premises. He still has his regular bodyguard team for outside appearances and events, but he has us in charge of this estate and has chosen not to know the extent of Blondie's obsession. Now we've had three instances of her inserting the dolls onto the property. This latest one shows signs of the potential for bodily harm."

Sophie nodded. "Her mutilating that doll is not a good sign. I think we should consult with a psychologist at this point. Jake, do you want me to set up a call to Dr. Kinoshita?"

The petite, capable Japanese psychologist did contract work for Security Solutions, and Sophie had come to respect the woman's expertise in matters of the mind.

"Good idea. Send her photos of everything and let's schedule a conference call with her tomorrow." Jake flicked a finger toward their younger teammates. "I want you two patrolling the grounds tonight. Walk a perimeter like I showed you, both inside and outside the compound, and check closely for any evidence you can find. Somehow Blondie's getting past the cameras, and I want to know how and catch her doing it."

Sophie could almost hear the inward groans the young men gave as they stood, inclined their heads respectfully, and left.

Sophie leaned toward Jake. "You're worried."

"I have a bad feeling about this. And every time I've had a bad feeling, something bad happens." He paused, met her eyes. "I had a bad feeling about you taking that Big Island case."

Sophie rubbed the tingling skin graft over the artificial cheekbone on the side of her face, rebuilt after she'd been shot. Jake had likely saved her life on that case. "You never told me about having feelings."

Jake's eyes weren't totally gray—they had an indigo ring around the iris, and his thick lashes would have been feminine on a softer face. Those eyes flared wider, and she glimpsed something dark and hot in them.

Uh-oh. She didn't mean to say that in any suggestive way. She tried not to give Jake any false signals. *They were friends and partners, nothing more, even more so now that she was with Connor.*

His voice was low. "I'm pretty sure you have an idea about my feelings."

Sophie looked down at her phone, a handy distraction. "I meant…your supposed prophetic moments."

"So, you're saying that you know what I'm saying."

Sophie looked up at him, her expression as blank as she could make it. "I don't understand what you mean. That sentence was very unclear."

Jake surged to his feet. "Never mind. Let me know when the conference is scheduled with Kinoshita. The guys have the grounds covered. You should go get some sleep." He scooped up the plastic figures and left.

———

BACK AT THE guest room she was staying in, Sophie was too unsettled to relax. She changed into running clothes. She wouldn't be able to get to sleep without exercise, and maybe she could spot something suspicious outside the compound. Jake didn't like her nighttime runs for safety reasons, but when she looked out the window, the gorgeous length of moonlit beach was empty, as usual.

She set her Glock in the drawer of the nightstand beside the bed in her room and picked up her phone and texted Jake per protocol: *"Going for a run. Too restless to sleep."*

"Want company?"

"No thanks."

Sophie slid the phone into her pocket, along with her Taser. Maui was, for the most part, one of the safest places in the United States crime-wise, but right now she had enemies. She walked out of the main house and down across the lawn, exiting through the Plexiglas gate.

Sophie hit her stride barefoot in the hard-packed sand near the water's edge. As they often did during her times alone, her thoughts turned to Todd Connor Remarkian, the enigmatic CEO of Security Solutions—the man she was dating.

Not that they'd had much time together.

Sophie daydreamed a bit as the metronome of her steps mixed with the gentle beat of the surf on the quiet beach. She'd finally committed her body and heart to someone, and the memories of their time together still made her chest tight with warm, tender feeling.

She and Connor had spent one unforgettable weekend together at the Hana Hotel before she had begun the current job at Shank Miller's a couple of weeks ago. They kept in touch via text message and long phone calls at night, but she missed him with a deep ache.

Hopefully, her role on the Miller job, installing, optimizing, and training the nanny cam AI software that tracked human patterns in the subject's house, would be over soon.

Sophie shook out her aching hand as she jogged. It was still a little sore, especially when overused, from a recent fracture to one of the bones in the back. For the most part, she'd quickly recovered from injuries sustained on her last assignment. But so far, life in the private sector was proving much more physically hazardous than her former career as an FBI agent.

The moon caressed the expanse of glittering black ocean. Palm trees created a jagged but graceful frame for the star-studded night sky. The smell of the sea, with its savor of salt and life, filled her nostrils. The mellow rhythms of slack-key guitar, that uniquely Hawaiian music, drifted down from one of the nearby hotels. The swish and retreat of gentle surf accompanied the beat of her footsteps as she ran. *Paradise.*

Sophie couldn't help missing her big yellow Lab, Ginger, on a night like this. Ginger loved a good night run on the beach, and it would have been perfect to be running with Connor, too, and his beautifully trained, dignified Doberman, Anubis. Ginger was staying with friends Marcella and Marcus on Oahu at their little cottage outside of Honolulu, and Marcus joked that they were never giving her back.

The attack, when it came, felt like being slammed out of nowhere by some dark force.

Sophie's body arched involuntarily, falling forward. A cry

died on her lips as she crashed onto the hard sand near the water's edge, her body twitching and spasming. All thought was shattered and disrupted, and blackness closed her eyes.

Chapter Three

Sophie came around to feel hands and bodies on either side of her, dragging her limp form along the beach.

A Taser. She had been tased—and it hurt way worse than she'd ever imagined. Her limbs were unresponsive and her skin crawled. Even her scalp tingled and burned. Her eyes rolled in her head and refused to focus—not that there was anything to make out but dark shapes and the sand beneath her.

"Hurry up," The man on her right said. "We don't want to be seen out here."

"She didn't look this heavy," the one on her left complained. Both were panting heavily as they half-dragged, half-carried Sophie's solidly muscular five-foot-nine, one-hundred-forty-pound body up the sloping beach.

Sophie let her head loll forward, trying to assess the situation. The electrical shock had disrupted her neural pathways and jangled every circuit in her body. She felt weak and disoriented, as intended, unable to fight back and felled by the element of surprise.

"I swear, he never said she was this heavy," the one on her

left complained again. *He.* This had to be an attempt to kidnap her by Assan Ang, her sadistic felon ex-husband! Yes, Sophie had powerful enemies—and one in particular. She was on her way to being tortured, raped, and killed.

Sophie dug her toes into the sand, creating drag, slowing the men down. The one on the left stumbled and grunted, eliciting a curse from the one on her right. *They were off-balance.* Sophie bent her knees and contracted her abs, dragging her legs forward. Calling on every reserve she had, she shot up to stand, ripping her arms out of their grip.

She was in no shape to fight two strong men. *Her best option was flight, and there was only one direction with any real possibility.* Sophie spun away and staggered toward the ocean, reeling and falling, scrambling up and propelling her body toward the water as fast as she could.

She barely heard the curses and cries behind her, but they were gaining. She was probably in better shape than her pursuers, if only her body could throw off enough of the effects of electrical shock to escape.

The ocean hitting her knees felt colder than Maui's water should be, but the wet chill sensation blasted the last of the fog from her brain. Sophie dove in, flinging herself forward with all her strength.

She couldn't let them hit her with the Taser again. Hopefully, the water would disable the weapon, not amplify it!

Sophie heard splashing behind her, but didn't slow down to see how close her pursuers might be. She just launched forward with everything she had, flailing her arms and kicking her feet, churning through the black water as fast as her weakened body would go. She swam straight out from shore toward the moonlit horizon.

Face down in the inky sea, Sophie found the rhythm of an overhand stroke, creating distance with every powerful pull of her arms as her strength returned.

She didn't slow until her lungs were burning and her arms

were limp as string. When she finally paused, lifting her head to look back toward shore, her eyes stung from the salt and her body trembled uncontrollably.

She shook the water from her eyes, gazing at the distant beach. A black line of palm trees and greenery lined the shore, highlighting the lit shapes of houses and the silver emptiness of the beach. Her pockets felt heavy with her ruined cell phone and her own useless Taser.

But not even her Glock would have protected her from the surprise attack she'd endured. Stupid to have been daydreaming about her boyfriend. There was no doubt in her mind who was behind the attack—*Assan.* She'd known the Hong Kong gangster had escaped federal custody, but had been lulled into sloppiness by no sign of him since the news of his escape.

Assan had sworn to kill her the last time he saw her, and she had no doubt he planned to do that—but in his own good time, when he'd tired of torturing her. The thought chilled her, sapping her energy. The inevitability of her death at his hands seemed to take her over, trying to pull her down into the black depths in which she swam.

Suicide would cheat Assan of his pleasure, and save herself pain.

"Ah, depression, my old friend. I wondered when I'd hear from you," she murmured, salt stinging her mouth as she spoke the words aloud.

Dr. Kinoshita had told Sophie to identify the depression's powerful thoughts to help distance them from herself. Over time, Sophie had come to recognize the distinct "sound" of those thoughts—and they came to her in her mother Pim Wat's flat, sad voice.

Sophie lay back in the water, letting her bare feet drift upward, spreading her arms to float as best she could. She gazed up into the vault of the sky. The moon on the horizon was almost as bright as dawn. The stars seemed close enough to touch. Perhaps it was the electrical shock, or the effect of an overdose of adrenaline, but it seemed like she could fall upward into the stars, and be absorbed into space.

Everything was just atoms, vibrating at different frequencies. She was a tiny part of it all, and separation was merely an illusion.

Not the voice of depression, this time. This was the voice of Spirit speaking within her. She was learning to recognize that, too.

The cold of the water penetrated, and Sophie rolled onto her belly, striking out for shore with a gentle breaststroke, trying not to imagine all of the creatures below her in the inky dark water, some of which might enjoy her as a snack. Little current or wave action impeded her progress back to shore, and for that she was grateful. She swam for an endless period before her feet touched the sandy bottom and she staggered up onto the sand, still a good way off from the estate.

But the beach was lit up with the floodlights Shank Miller hated. The dark silhouettes of Jake and their two men moved along the beach toward her, flashlights in their hands.

Sophie straightened, pushing her tired, sopping body forward through the shallow water. She raised her arms, waving. "Over here!"

———

ANTIGUA, Shank Miller's property manager and chef, handed Sophie a mug of strong Thai tea. "Here. Drink this."

The china rim of the cup chattered against Sophie's teeth as she sipped, wrapped in a towel and seated on one of the canvas-covered couches in Miller's living room. She kept her eyes down as Jake sat across from her on an ottoman.

"Sophie." Jake squeezed her forearm with a big hand. She raised her eyes reluctantly to his.

"I'm sorry. I shouldn't have gone out alone for a run."

"An accurate assessment. I believe I told you some time ago

that you can't afford that kind of risk until Ang is in custody." Jake's eyes were blued steel.

Sophie nodded and sipped her tea. Her hands were steadier. "You were right. Try not to gloat."

"This is too serious for gloating. I'll save that for the little stuff, like when I beat you in the ring." They practiced mixed martial arts sparring several times weekly to keep up combat skills. "So, I called your cop friend, Lei. She's on her way to interview you about the attack."

"I appreciate that. Lei knows the story." The idea of telling a random unknown police officer her long and painful history with Assan Ang made Sophie's stomach cramp. "I should call Marcella, too. And Connor. I just need a few more minutes to pull myself together. And, I'll need a new phone."

"I have an extra burner you can have, and you can download your contacts list." Jake squeezed her arm. She'd forgotten his hand still gripped her. He stood and began to pace with that restless energy that was such a part of him. "I'm going to review the surveillance footage from the cameras looking down the beach. See if your wannabe kidnappers were caught on camera."

"Good idea. Thank you."

Jake strode off as Antigua entered, bringing her familiar aroma of coconut and gardenia. The woman's café latte skin gleamed in the lamplight as she held out a fresh towel to Sophie. "I'm thinking a hot shower might feel good before you have to tell your story to the cops." Her warm voice was compassionate. "I know I wouldn't want to be sitting around in soaked, salty clothes if I were you."

Sophie rose from the couch and took the towel gratefully, handing the chef her empty mug. "Yes, thanks. You are absolutely right about that."

Under the fall of water in the little bathroom attached to her guest suite, Sophie assessed herself for damage. The Taser had struck her between her shoulder blades. The prongs had dug into skin revealed by her skimpy running top and the area felt sore. She still felt some residual weakness, and the thump of an approaching headache—but she was unharmed otherwise.

She was damn lucky to have gotten away.

Assan was going to be more crafty and prepared next time. He would find some new way to attack her when her guard was down. She remembered his mind games all too well, punishments ranging from subtle to overt. Her escape would enrage him; he would look for a way to make her suffer.

The depression beat its dark wings, urging her to give up, give in, and let whatever might come happen. *"You always lose, Sophie. You are just unlucky, always have been. Doomed. You might as well give up."*

But she had so much to live for. A new relationship with an amazing man, friends, and a truly great dog. She looked down at the delicate curlicued Thai writing on the insides of her arms: *hope* and *respect, power* and *truth.* Down the outsides of her thighs: *courage* and *freedom.* Circling her navel in tiny writing were *love, joy,* and *bliss.* These words were her mantra, her destiny—not the crippling negativity of the depression.

She'd escaped and she had beaten Assan before—and she could do it again. She *would* do it again, and ultimately, she'd find a way to make sure he never hurt her, or anyone she loved, ever again. And she might have to do it herself.

Sophie met with Sergeant Leilani Texeira and her longtime partner Pono Kaihale in Shank Miller's den, a masculine room sporting a pool table and video game console as well as a small home theater area.

Lei enfolded Sophie in a hug. Her friend's curly brown hair tickled Sophie's nose, and her athletic body, clad in the usual tank top with cotton jacket and jeans, felt wiry and petite in Sophie's arms. "I'm sorry to have to come see you for this reason."

"It's always good to see you, Lei, no matter the circumstances."

"Likewise." The women smiled at each other, and Lei gestured to the deep armchair under a masculine, green shaded lamp. "Just begin at the beginning. Pono will tape this, so you don't have to repeat anything. And if we have questions, we'll let you know."

After Pono set up the recording with date, time, and people present, Sophie started in. "I believe the kidnappers were sent by my ex-husband, Assan Ang."

Conscious of laying the groundwork for the investigation by sharing background, Sophie told them her history with Ang in brief, detached terms.

The arranged marriage in Thailand when she was nineteen. The five years in Hong Kong when she had lived as a captive in their apartment, allowed out only on Assan's arm for social reasons or to attend college, where she'd studied computer science. Her escape from Ang, a carefully engineered plan that had brought her to the United States and into the FBI, who'd headhunted Sophie in Hong Kong for her language and tech abilities. A brief synopsis of her five-year career as a tech agent in the FBI. The case that had led her to uncover Ang's elaborate plot to recapture her. The brutal showdown between them that resulted in his arrest. And finally, Ang's escape from federal custody during his extradition back to Hong Kong.

"I'm sorry to make you go through all of that again," Lei said. Her brown eyes were compassionate.

So were Pono's, as the sturdy Hawaiian man nodded in support. "It's important that we have all the facts on record as we move ahead to try to capture Ang." Pono's big brown hands dwarfed the stylus he used to take notes on his tablet. "You're here working on a security detail for Shank Miller. Is there any chance that this attack is related to that case, instead?"

"I don't believe so. There a Detective Cruz with MPD who is handling the criminal tracking of the stalking case on Miller. This attempt to kidnap me does not match anything about that case."

"We didn't think so," Lei agreed. "We just have to explore every possibility. We'll contact Cruz so we don't duplicate any efforts."

"I wouldn't be surprised if this crazy fan calling herself Blondie doesn't make some sort of attempt to capture Shank in the not-too-distant future," Sophie said. "But as of now, I believe tonight's attack was directed only at me. I've been expecting something from Assan. He promised to kill me the next time we met. But I suspect he will keep me alive for a while first, to…" Sophie's throat closed. She was unable to speak of the sexual and other tortures she suspected Ang had planned for her.

Pono cleared his throat and looked away, clearly uncomfortable, but Lei met Sophie's eyes squarely. "Staying inside this compound and going out only with an escort seem like pretty reasonable precautions. I'm surprised Jake let you go jogging at night, alone."

"Jake's not in charge of how I spend my personal time," Sophie said, irritation flushing her neck.

"Partners look out for each other," Pono said, with a head nod to Lei. "I've had a few things to say to Lei over the years about both her personal life *and* how she was handling her work. And she's never short on opinions about me, either."

Sophie swallowed, looking down at her hands. "You two have a different dynamic than Jake and I."

Lei cleared her throat. "As you know, I'm the FBI liaison on Maui, so I'll get in touch with the Oahu Bureau office to work on the investigation into Ang's whereabouts. We'll make sure the Oahu team is updated on this latest incident, and try to get some manpower over here to check whether he is on Maui. We'll also be looking for the two thugs who tried to grab you. Good job getting away. I've been tased myself, and it's no fun." Lei patted Sophie's shoulder. "The good news is you'll be fine in the morning. Get some rest."

"I'll try." Sophie staggered to her room, wishing she'd just listened to Jake and gone to bed hours ago. Jake had left the burner phone for her on the bureau, and she took the time to download her contacts—but calling Connor and Marcella felt too exhausting. She fell asleep with the phone in her hand, curled close to her body.

Chapter Four

S ophie woke to knocking on her door. She knuckled her eyes, slipping into the silk robe embroidered with dragons her aunt had sent from Thailand. She opened the door. "Yes?"

"There's someone here to see you. I wanted to make sure he is authorized before I let him in." Antigua's dark brown eyes were concerned. "His name is Todd Remarkian."

Sophie's pulse picked up immediately. "Of course, let him in. He is our boss—the CEO of Security Solutions."

Even as she turned away from the door to get dressed, Sophie wondered why she hadn't identified Todd, who went by Connor in private, as her boyfriend. *Was she afraid of saying those words?*

She dressed quickly in her usual work outfit of black yoga pants and button-down shirt. There was nothing to be done about her thick, curly hair, matted from the ordeal last night and sleeping on it wet. She missed the days of her short MMA buzz cut for that reason.

She checked her face in the mirror as she slicked on colored lip balm. Connor had told her many times that she was beautiful in spite of the unevenness created by the facial prosthetic and the scar bisecting her cheekbone, marking a skin graft stitched up into her hairline. The change in her appearance from the gunshot wound still jarred Sophie whenever she looked in the mirror.

Connor was talking to Jake in the rock star's spacious living room, and broke off when he caught sight of her. He strode across the broad expanse of polished teak floor to embrace her, pulling her in close. "Thank God you're okay."

Sophie closed her eyes and breathed him in, savoring the strength of his arms, his warm hard body against hers. She fit well against him, and reveled in that. He tipped her chin up with one hand and kissed her, right in front of Jake, Antigua, and the rest of their team.

Connor didn't have any trouble with their relationship status.

Sophie gave his chest a gentle push. "I'm fine. Lei was right. Nothing cures tasing like a good night's sleep."

Connor pushed a hand through his short blond hair. Sea-colored eyes studied her intently as a frown stitched a line between his brows. His Aussie accent was broad with distress. "Why didn't you call me last night? Why did I have to hear about what happened from Jake?"

Sophie glanced over Connor's shoulder to see Jake heading for the nearest exit, Antigua in his wake. The two security operatives had also vanished.

"I'm sorry. I was so tired that I didn't have the energy to make another call and have to…"

Have to explain her ill-advised choice to take a run on the beach alone at night.

Have to relive the whole harrowing experience one more time.

Have to deal with Connor's emotional reaction.

What did it mean that calling Connor had not felt like something supportive, but like one more thing that would exhaust her?

Connor squeezed the back of her neck. "I had to see you and know that you were okay after I got Jake's call last night. I tried your phone, but it was turned off." The vibration in his tone told her he was trying not to be angry.

"My phone got ruined in the ocean. I have a new one." She pulled it out and texted him her new number.

"Are you up for a little walk on the beach?"

"That would be perfect." Sophie reached out, took his hand. She rubbed her thumb over the callus between his thumb and forefinger, the place where the neck of his violin rested. Touching that roughened patch of skin reminded her of all the things she admired about him—not least of which was his willingness to openly care for her when he was such a private and guarded person.

The ocean in front of the mansion was still cool with early morning, the purplish bulk of Haleakala casting a long blue shadow over pristine sand populated only by a few early morning joggers and dog walkers. The wind Maui was so famous for had not yet risen, and the sea was as calm and smooth as mercury, reflecting the sky and a few lazy white clouds. Mynah birds, waking up in the coconut palms fringing the beach, chattered noisily and mourning doves cooed. Sophie twined her fingers with Connor's as they walked barefoot down the beach. "I should have called you right away. Before the cops came."

"I would have appreciated that." Connor's voice was tight. "I wanted to hear it from you."

"I understand. But I'm sure Jake had all the facts, and his brain wasn't scrambled from a Taser."

"I never want to hear from Jake about you, ever again," Connor said flatly. Sophie stiffened at the steely note in his voice. "Jake has feelings for you. I am reassigning him."

Sophie stopped, digging her heels into the sand. She let go of Connor's hand and turned to face him. "So, this is what happens when you date the boss. People warned me that it would interfere with my job, and it has."

"That's not the only change I'm laying down today. I have a lead on Ang, and I'm handling the situation."

Sophie glared at him. "We've talked about this. He's mine to take out."

"Not up to you anymore. I let you have your chance, and he almost got you."

Sophie looked down, because she couldn't bear to see the expression in Connor's eyes—the note of fury and anguish in his voice was more than enough. He went on. "Don't be stubborn. Admit he's out ahead of us right now, and we need to bag him by any means. And I have the means."

Sophie whirled and strode down the beach. She could hear his footsteps following, and she sped up. She was too angry to speak. *The men in her life thought they knew better, thought she couldn't handle her own business, when she'd proved over and over again that she was both competent and deadly.*

Whatever sloppiness might have occurred up until now was over.

She turned back to face Connor at last. She took in all of him visually: the light of morning falling over Haleakala, striking his shoulder like a lance, lighting his blond head with gold like a warrior's helmet, caressing the planes of his face, molding over his muscled body. "If you do this, we're done."

Connor had halted too. His gaze was hot and determined. "I'll just have to trust that this is one more thing we can get past eventually. Are you going to walk off again and make me follow you? Or can we head back and get on with this manhunt?"

"Give me your lead on Assan," Sophie snapped. "And I will use DAVID to find him."

"Because that has worked so well."

Their gazes clashed. Sophie tightened her lips. *Whatever anger she felt right now needed to be put aside in favor of finding her ex.* They fell into step walking back to the beachfront mansion, but Sophie kept a couple of feet of space between them, and Connor shoved his hands into his pockets.

"Assan is bound to have left some trace of himself online now that he is using hired assistance. I'm sure Lei and the FBI will have more to work with, as will I. So, what's that lead?" Sophie said.

"Just let me do what I need to do. Don't make this about us."

Sophie didn't like his tone, or his attitude. She narrowed her eyes. "No. I don't need or want your help. On this or any other case." She did not know when that realization had hardened into crystal clarity, but it had. "Give me that lead!"

Connor stared at her for another moment. His face might have been carved from stone. He turned and walked briskly toward the mansion. Clearly, he wasn't sharing his intel with her.

Sophie watched him go. He reached the end of Miller's compound, and the almost invisible Plexiglas gate opened for him like magic.

Like she had opened for him.

It had taken time and effort to lure her in and break down her resistance and caution, but in the end, she had yielded to him. Let herself be hopeful for a future.

Let herself love him.

Had she made the right choice? Was there any way to go back?

Her body tingled, remembering how good they'd been together that one weekend, and her chest felt heavy and sore at the thought of goodbye.

This was even worse than when Alika dumped her and left for Kaua'i. *She was such a fool.*

Sophie broke into a jog and moved briskly down the beach, fighting off depressive thoughts that swirled in to fan her self-doubt.

She entered the house a half hour later and was surprised to see Jake standing outside the den that had been their former security headquarters, arms crossed on his chest, face serious.

He was guarding someone inside that room.

Sophie had finally relaxed from her confrontation with Connor, but now sweat pooled in an itchy line down the back of her shirt from the heat of the run. She couldn't wait to be alone and sort through what was going on, couldn't wait to get into the shower and then back into the cool dim computer area to check DAVID's data caches that were scrubbing the internet for traces of Assan. Even stacking and sorting the behavior patterns they had been recording using Security Solutions' AI surveillance program seemed appealing, because she couldn't wait to be back in her comfort zone. "Did Mr. Miller get back or something?"

Jake's lips tightened, his gray eyes unreadable. "Lei and Pono are interviewing someone."

"Good. It's about time you had a break in the Blondie case."

Jake's expression didn't change, and now Sophie frowned. "Is the interview in there about *my* case?"

Jake shrugged and looked off over her shoulder. His body language sent a clear message.

"Well, it's apparent you're not going to tell me what this is about, so I might as well take a shower. Let me know when I'm to be honored by your confidence. *Partner.*" Sophie walked stiffly past him down the hall.

She had worked so hard for calm, and it was gone in a moment.

Chapter Five

Washing up and changing back at her room, Sophie considered who Lei and Pono might be interviewing in the den. Maybe they'd got a lead on someone who had leaked information about her movements at the house to the would-be kidnappers; the fact that those thugs could grab her when they had seemed awfully convenient.

Sophie felt her belly hollow as she considered the various staff people who might have been compromised: Antigua, either of their two young operatives, Jesse or Ronnie, Pepe, the groundskeeper. Even someone at Security Solutions off-site, with remote access to the nanny cam software that was always recording her movements around the estate, could have leaked her location.

On the other hand, this new development could be about the Blondie case—but if so, she couldn't think of any reason why Jake wouldn't just tell her what that was.

Sophie needed a good strong cup of tea after this rough start to the day. She had brought her own tea, special ordered from an import company, and carrying the small paper bag, she headed into the heart of Miller's mansion, the gigantic state-of-the-art kitchen.

Antigua was washing something up at the sink, her toned arms deep in suds. "You're late for your morning tea." She gestured with her regal head to a carafe resting on the marble sideboard. "I made you some hours ago."

"Thank you." Sophie felt a lump in her throat, a combined reaction to the woman's thoughtfulness and relief that it wasn't Antigua being questioned in that closed room. "My boyfriend Todd and I had a talk, then I took a beach run to clear my head. I'm ready for anything now." Her smile felt automatic, a mask to hide her turbulent anxiety. Calling Connor her "boyfriend" still felt awkward, odd. They were too mature, and the relationship too intense, for the word to feel like a fit.

"Well, he's still here, talking with the cops. I don't know what they wanted to talk to him about, what he might have known about your attack or even the Blondie case, but they're all closed up in the den."

Sophie hid the tightening of her abs in response to this news by busying her hands with pouring the tea.

What could Lei and Pono be talking to Connor about?

There were too many possibilities, and few of them were good.

Sophie did not let her mind speculate, keeping her voice level and matter of fact. "Okay. Tell him I'm heading out to the security center and perhaps he can stop by on his way out. When is Mr. Miller getting back?"

"I spoke with him this morning. He is staying over in Quebec for another concert, but then, he should be home for a week or so."

"I hope we get a break on the Blondie case before he returns." Sophie nodded to Antigua as she walked out. She wrapped her hands around the mug, hoping it would warm her as she hurried back across the length of the mansion, out the side door, and over elegant embedded flagstones to the guest cottage where the security center was located.

She dismissed Ronnie, who'd been keeping watch on the monitors. Sitting down in the comfortable leather office chair in front of the multiple screens surveilling the property, Sophie tried to keep her mind from wandering back to the den and Connor.

Maybe they were talking to him about Security Solutions' role, and response to her attack. After all, Connor was her boss, even if only technically. Could it be about their relationship? The lead he'd uncovered about Assan?

She refused to consider that they might know about the Ghost. She was the only one who knew about the Ghost.

She would know soon enough.

Sophie wrestled her thoughts back into focus by putting on headphones and filling her ears with classical music as she pulled up the complicated algorithm of the nanny cam surveillance software and began to assess the emergent patterns.

Unfortunately, all of the data she'd gathered would be outdated when Shank Miller returned. The whole point of the software was to automate and identify abnormal behavior patterns. When tuned up correctly, the software was much more accurate than hired watchmen. Sophie hoped getting it set up might not only protect Miller more economically than a large human staff, but it could lead to a break in the Blondie case.

Sophie had enough data about the rest of the household's "normal" life patterns to run the program effectively, but Miller hadn't been home enough to integrate his patterns into the overall picture, and the software would need to be trained all over again when Miller took up residence.

That was a problem.

But maybe now she could take a break and go back to Oahu and see Ginger while Miller did that last concert in Quebec.

And see Connor, and work things out with him.

Connor wouldn't like her going back to her off-the-grid

apartment and alternate identity as Mary Watson, but until she knew better, Sophie hoped that Assan didn't know about that identity. Mary Watson existed to give her a layer of protection and anonymity, make her harder to find.

Sophie assembled the nanny cam analysis into a single report and contacted Kendall Bix, her immediate supervisor and VP of operations at Security Solutions. She wanted to get the okay to go back to Oahu before she had to talk to Jake about it.

Bix was noncommittal on the phone. "I need to check in with Jake. And Dr. Kinoshita just let me know she's coming over for a consult on the Miller case. I think you should be present for that, and afterward we can talk."

"When is the doctor arriving?" Sophie had a pen ready to jot down the date, time, and flight number.

She was still on the phone with Bix when the door banged open, and she spun to face the threat.

Connor stood in the doorway, aqua eyes ablaze and hair mussed. He strode back and forth rapidly while she wrapped up the call. His muscles were pumped, and anger seemed to shiver in the air around him. The minute she got off the phone he grabbed her by the arms, pulling her up out of the chair. "Hey!" she exclaimed, but he kissed her anyway.

Sophie stiffened, pulling back, twisting her face away. He held her close, then let go abruptly, stroking her arms. "Sorry about that. I just needed to hold you a minute."

"I don't like being manhandled," Sophie said. "You know why."

"Damn it. Yes, I know. I just couldn't bear to leave with discord between us."

"That didn't help," Sophie said.

Connor threw up his hands, stalking away. She'd never seen him so agitated. "This is so difficult! And it's going to get even harder." He spun to face her, pinning her with a hard, blue gaze.

"You're going to hear things about me. Don't believe what they tell you."

"What's this about?" Sophie frowned. "What the hell is going on?"

"I wasn't supposed to speak to you at all. I have to go. They'll be here any minute. Just believe me—I had nothing to do with what they're saying. I'll be in touch." He whirled, and the door slammed closed behind him.

A moment later, she heard the roar of the white Security Solutions SUV Connor drove leaving the estate.

What was happening? The nagging, prickling hurt of the way they'd parted brushed along her nerves, making her stomach knot, and the sight of Connor barely hanging onto self-control was not reassuring.

A knock came from the door. Sophie answered it. Lei stood on the step, Pono a looming but benign presence behind her shoulder. Both of their faces were uncharacteristically serious.

"We need to speak with you about your case. And something else. Where can we be guaranteed confidentiality?" Lei asked.

Sophie gestured to the cluttered dining room table inside the cottage, site of many a team meeting. "The men sweep the house and grounds for bugs twice a week, and the last time was yesterday. The biggest possible interruption is Jake, and if you've dealt with him, we should be fine."

Sophie knew it was bad when the two didn't even smile. Lei just made a motion with her head, and Pono locked the door behind them.

Sophie cleared off the cluttered dining room table with quick, jerky movements. "Who were you interviewing in the den?" she asked, to get things started.

"We had questions for your boyfriend, Todd Remarkian." Lei sat down at the table, Pono beside her, and opened a file.

Sophie kept her face neutral, hiding her apprehension. "Is this something to do with my attack? Or with the situation with Blondie?"

"Neither." Pono spoke this time, lacing thick fingers together and gazing at her over them with soulful brown eyes. "There's an investigation going on at the FBI. They are looking into Remarkian for shady online dealings through Security Solutions."

Sophie's stomach lurched and tightened as she sat down slowly, facing them. *This had to be something to do with the Ghost.* But how had they detected the Ghost's activities?

"As you know, I'm the FBI contact for Maui," Lei said. "Technically, this isn't a case for Pono to be involved with, but I got clearance since I needed backup for the interview with Remarkian." Lei blew out a breath, shook her head, and made eye contact with Sophie. "There is an investigation into allegations that Remarkian is involved in some illegal online activities. An agent was killed not long ago, and there are those who think he was behind it."

Sophie gasped. "No. That's impossible." *They were onto the Ghost—and thought he was involved in the death of an agent?* This was worse than anything she'd dared imagine. Connor would never be involved with something like that…*unless the agent was dirty.*

"I'm sorry about this." Lei's tilted, warm brown eyes were serious as she gazed at Sophie. "You two are dating. I hate to throw a spoke in the wheel of your first big relationship since Alika…but these are serious concerns. Is there anything that worries you about his activities? About his online presence?"

Sophie stood up in agitation. She shoved her hands into her pockets, and paced. She had to buy time and get more information. "Where is this coming from? Who called you from Oahu?"

"Ken Yamada. My former partner in the FBI. You've worked cases with him, too. He told me he's had an eye on Todd since the disappearance of Sheldon Hamilton on your last case together. And I believe you know all about that case." Lei's gaze was implacable when Sophie glanced at her friend.

"I can't believe Todd would ever be mixed up in…murder." The word stuck in Sophie's throat. *What a lie.* The Ghost dealt his version of justice evenhandedly, with no regard for title or position. The Ghost believed in matching the severity of the crime with the severity of the punishment. If this agent was dead at the hand of the Ghost, the man had done something really terrible.

But Connor had told her to believe in him, that he wasn't involved with what they were accusing him of.

"I can't talk with you about this," Sophie said abruptly. "It's a conflict of interest for me."

Lei frowned, surprise in her raised brows. "What? You know something."

"I cannot participate in this investigation at this time," Sophie said woodenly. "I have to check some things out. I will get back to you when I'm ready to share. If I'm ready to share. Otherwise, you can subpoena me and I'll speak to you with a lawyer present."

Sophie's stomach churned as the faces of her friends stiffened and went cold. Finally, Lei stood up. "Okay. I know it won't do any good to drag you down to the station or something like that. This is a very sensitive situation, and we are all aware of that. I'm sorry even to have to put these thoughts into your mind about Todd, Sophie, but better sooner than later if there's truth in it, right?" She cocked her head with a sad smile.

Sophie could not smile back. "You are correct. If we can be done, now, I need to make some phone calls."

Chapter Six

Thinking about the report from the two operatives who had failed to capture his wife filled Assan with familiar rage. *She was so much stronger than she used to be.* It didn't pay to underestimate her ability to evade him.

But that strength would also make her capture so much more satisfying.

He had to find a way to punish her. She would expect it—she'd know she'd earned his wrath. And once she'd been chastened, he'd find a subtler way to capture and control her.

Assan looked out the window at the view of ocean and sky: *another boring tropical seascape.* The climate was nice here, not as hot as Hong Kong—but the slow pace of life, the celebratory mood of the people in his area, the need for concealment—all of it irritated him. He would be here only as long as it took to get his hands on her, and to do the business they had together.

A slow smile spread across Assan's face as he considered an idea. He picked up the phone to contact his man on Oahu.

———

KEN YAMADA HAD a cool voice on the phone, carrying the lilt of someone who had grown up in Hawaii. "This is Special Agent Yamada."

"Ken? It's Sophie."

Lei and Pono had left Sophie alone at last, and after turning over the surveillance cams to Ronnie again, Sophie was back in the guest room inside Shank Miller's, throwing her clothing and belongings into a duffel.

"Sophie." Ken sighed, and Sophie could clearly picture her former colleague's severely handsome, ascetic face, the way he pinched the bridge of his nose. "Lei and Pono must have talked to you."

"Yes, they did." Sophie rolled each item of her simple clothing into a tight bundle and packed it into the bag. "And as a friend, I'm wondering why you didn't call me yourself as soon as you suspected Todd Remarkian might be mixed up with the vigilante we investigated on that Security Solutions case."

"I wanted… Damn it, Sophie, I wanted something good for you. And Todd seemed like a good thing. But then we got some new intel, and I thought the news—and the questions—would be better coming from Lei, in person, than from me on the phone."

Sophie sat abruptly on the end of the bed, her legs giving out. "You really think he killed an agent?"

A long pause. Finally, "Not necessarily. But I think Remarkian's involved with that Ghost character we uncovered during that first Security Solutions case we worked."

"Tell me everything."

"I can't." Ken's voice was laden with regret. "You know I have nothing but respect for you, Sophie. But we can't disclose an ongoing investigation to a possible witness. You know that as much as anyone."

"We're dating. I've slept with him!" Sophie exclaimed, balling a fist and pressing it against her aching stomach. She and Ken had forged a bond over their cases together; she knew about his orientation and trusted his quiet integrity. "Tell me I didn't just make the hugest mistake of my life."

"I wish I could say for sure, Soph." His gentle tone made tears prickle her eyes. "But I'm pretty sure your biggest mistake was marrying Assan Ang."

"Ha. You are correct on that one." Sophie shook her head, stood up. Paced. She returned to rolling a pair of yoga pants and stuffing them into her bag. "Assan's still trying to get to me."

"I know. Lei informed the office. And we're looking for him, as I'm sure you know. I wish I could come over and search for him there on Maui myself, but I'm stuck here on a case. We want Ang in custody as much as you do."

"He's off the grid. Which is where I need to go also." Sophie rattled off the burner phone number. "I'm returning to my Mary Watson identity and I'll be offline, except for this phone, until he's captured."

"That's not a good idea, Sophie. You should stay where you are, make use of your secure and reinforced location." Ken paused. "I'm sure your partners at Security Solutions would agree."

"I don't much care what anyone thinks right now." Sophie's neck felt hot. "I was attacked by professionals within a hundred yards of this supposedly secure location, where we have continued to receive objects harassing our client. Very disturbing objects, with threatening messages. So, you'll pardon me if I don't feel very secure here. I may actually be adding risk to our client, as well. I'll do better on my own." She ended the call.

———

THE CASH-ONLY HOSTEL in the little beachfront town of Paia on Maui's north shore was just a place to throw her duffel down and crash while she worked on finding Assan. She'd stayed in

Ma`alea on her last job, but varying patterns were important in escaping detection.

Jake, of course, had not agreed with her plan. "I can keep you safe. I can make sure he doesn't come after you again. That's what we're doing for Shank Miller. How could hiding by yourself be better?"

"Jake, I'm not going to discuss this with you. I'm a liability to your surveillance detail here. I might actually bring danger to Miller in his home, and that's the last thing he needs." Sophie had faced Jake as he blocked the exit of the mansion, ripped and intimidating in a workout tee with the neck and sleeves torn off. Even in casual clothes he was wearing a weapon in a shoulder holster.

"I need you here." Gray eyes burned holes in her.

"No, you don't. I've prepped a report and left it for you. The AI software is as trained as I can get it without Miller in residence. The next phase begins when he is here for at least a week, and the cameras can record his activity for analysis. I am leaving, and here's the only number where you can reach me. Call if you need anything for work." She pressed a Post-it note into his hand and brushed by him, out the door.

For a second, she thought he was actually going to try to physically stop her, but the moment passed. She could still hear his voice, low and forceful. "Be careful. *Please.*"

She *was* being careful. She knew how to spot a tail, and hadn't detected one when she left Miller's—but to make sure he hadn't tracked her out of the compound, she'd returned the rental car and taken a cab to Paia. She'd go back and pick up another rental tomorrow.

Sophie looked around the bare room with its sturdy, hand-made queen bed built of two-by-fours. The plinking sound of a dripping faucet echoed from the tiny bathroom. The palms outside rushed and sang in the ever-present Maui wind as Sophie set up some of her own security measures: a detachable extra lock, and a tiny motion-activated security cam that fed to her phone.

At the sink, Sophie cut off most of her hair with her nail scissors. Soon the sink was full of fluffy, dark brown curls, hair she'd tried to grow out for months to hide the scar on her face and up into her hairline. *A vain effort—it had never worked, anyway.* She eyed her stark reflection in the mirror with a grimace.

With her hair shortened, she was able to fit on a long black wig. She put on some makeup and red lipstick.

Wearing hair to her waist, a pretty feminine dress, and modish black-framed glasses, Sophie Ang disappeared and Mary Watson took her place.

Deepening shadow seeped into the luminous evening sky as Sophie donned a pair of sturdy sandals and a sun hat. Her laptop in a jute bag under her arm, she headed out into the festive little town with its brightly colored shops and warm, crowded streets.

Trapped sunlight from the waning day radiated heat from the sidewalk up her legs, but Sophie was well-covered by a pair of exercise shorts under her dress. *Nothing got in the way of her mobility.* Wearing a swirly skirt had almost lost her a fight with a deadly perpetrator while dressed in her Mary Watson disguise.

Sophie walked to her favorite Maui coffee and crêpe restaurant, Café des Amis. Seated at one of the bamboo tables, an iced tea at her elbow, she booted up the secure satellite hookup on her laptop and routed her connection through a series of Virtual Private Network nodes, assuring her online anonymity. Her back to the corner of the restaurant, the brim of her sun hat down, Sophie left her earbuds in place but turned off, staying alert to the ebb and flow of people around her.

She didn't think Assan would try anything in a crowded venue like this, but she'd already learned it didn't pay to get complacent.

Sophie activated her rogue software program and combed the Internet using DAVID's powerful search engine, looking for any trace of information on the case involving the Ghost that had brought the FBI out to interview Connor. There was nothing new in the cache she'd had gathering intel on him for the last month. *Perhaps their talks had made a difference, and Connor was rethinking his vigilante role.*

But more likely, he had gotten wind of the FBI's investigation and was lying low until things blew over. He'd told her he was not going to stop his mission for her, or for anyone.

Sophie had uncovered his secret some time ago, and shelved her reservations about it in the face of their overwhelming attraction to each other. She'd always worried, though, that the Ghost vigilante carried the seeds of destruction for their relationship.

Sophie found a small story, almost buried, referring to the death of a twice-decorated Washington FBI agent— "under circumstances that the agency has refused to comment on." Neither name nor photo identified the agent in question. She dragged and dropped the snippet of news into a new cache file, labeled to monitor that specific case.

DAVID operated on search terms, so she generated several trackable ones to watch for online activity on the case.

Now to look for Assan. Sophie switched to the search caches she'd set up to troll for online trace of her ex, and her brows snapped together to see a digital footprint from one of Assan's financial accounts associated with an art gallery in Lahaina.

One of Assan's favorite access codes had been used to facilitate a large money transfer from a Hong Kong account to the upscale art gallery. Assan was on the FBI's most wanted list, and the only reason DAVID had twigged to this clue was that Sophie had input all the codes she remembered his using as part of DAVID's search keywords protocol.

Even as she looked, the digital trace erased itself.

Sophie pulled up the Paradise Treasures Gallery website, a chill sensation tripping fingers up her spine.

Assan's assets were supposed to be frozen as part of the

crackdown on his drug smuggling, but Sophie was not so naïve that she believed the FBI and Interpol had been able to find all of his accounts.

But she had this one clue, not one the FBI or Interpol would have been able to intercept, and it tied Assan to a location right here on Maui. And there was only one reason Assan would be here, out of all the places in the world where he could hide: *he was still trying to capture her.*

But not if she got to him first.

Could this be a trap? But if so, there was no way to know without checking it out, since the access code was the only lead she had. It was a pretty subtle clue, and Assan didn't know about DAVID's abilities unless he had a mole in the FBI or Security Solutions.

But no. She had to operate as if Ang knew about DAVID, knew what she would know, and might be setting up a trap. But this was also the first solid clue she'd had since his escape from federal custody.

She had to act on it, and she would. *Tomorrow.*

Twilight brought a waitress to light a candle on Sophie's table. "Do you want to order something to eat?"

Sophie indulged in a savory crêpe, finished her tea, and walked back through the streets to the hostel. Her eyes scanned everywhere for threats as her hand rested on Mary Watson's straw bag containing the laptop—and her Glock.

But she saw no one but happy tourists and preoccupied locals, and heard nothing but the swish of cars, barking of dogs, and shushing of coconut palms. The chatter of mynahs in a mango tree as they prepared to sleep caught her attention briefly, but her mind was preoccupied.

She was ready to talk to Connor. She needed to talk to him.

Sophie unlocked the humble hostel's room, her hand already on the new burner phone she was using. She called Connor's private cell. The phone rang and rang, ending in a mechanical voice mail. He wouldn't answer because he didn't recognize the number. Neither of them ever answered unknown numbers.

Sophie cleared her throat, deepened her voice, and covered her mouth with her hand to distort it further, broadening her British accent. "This is Mary Watson. You can reach me at this number regarding that matter we discussed."

Connor would be home in his well-appointed Pendragon Arches apartment. He'd probably be on his computers, or maybe he was practicing his violin. Maybe he was running on the beach with Anubis, or doing overhead presses on the home gym he kept in his hidden office.

Sophie felt a pulse of desire, thinking of him, of what he was doing. She hated the Ghost and its hold on Connor, but she loved that it was him, too.

And now the Ghost had come back to haunt them, as she'd always feared it would.

Chapter Seven

The burner rang, vibrating on the cheap pressboard nightstand like a bug in a bottle as she unloaded the straw bag, and she answered it. "Connor! Thanks for calling me back."

"Where are you?" His voice was tense, pressured.

"Somewhere safe." She glanced around the unprepossessing room of the hostel. "I hope."

"I'm still on Maui. Let me come to you." His voice softened. "Please. I need to see you."

"Yes," she breathed out a tension she hadn't known she held. "Watch for surveillance, okay? And …look like someone else."

"Of course." That being asked to wear a disguise didn't faze him a bit almost made Sophie smile. *They were certainly two of a kind in some ways.* She gave a location to meet in case their transmission was picked up.

Sophie walked the short distance to the beach park at Paia Bay, a moth-eaten patch of sunblasted grass marked by a colorfully painted cinder block bathroom and a basketball court. The nearby youth center was lit up for a skateboard event, and cars clustered willy-nilly around the area, all good camouflage for a clandestine meeting.

Sophie walked across the expanse of the park, and up a slight berm crowned with ironwood trees, alert to any followers. She took a spot in the shadow under the trees to watch the comings and goings in the park, glancing down onto the beach leading into the shallow bay. Moonlight glittered on waves beating on the sand, expending themselves over and over, a heartbeat that filled the background along with tinny rock music from the youth event.

Sophie scanned for Connor. They'd made a game of this before, in less serious circumstances, trying to sneak up on each other in some public place or tail each other. She spotted him, a slouching figure with a ball cap pulled low, walking with a group of teens—and then he jumped on one of the other kids' boards at the sidewalk and skated off.

No, that was him, the bent-over, bearded tourist…but under the streetlamp, the disguise held up.

"Sophie."

She jumped and whirled. Connor had come up from the sea, wearing a wetsuit, a board under his arm, his face hidden by a blond beard.

"Night surfing." Sophie smiled. "Good one. You surprised me."

"I have to work hard to beat the best." Connor reached her and lifted the short-brimmed straw hat she wore to kiss her. The beard tickled wet on her cheeks.

She laughed, giving the whiskers a gentle tug. "No one would identify you in this."

"Nor you, Mary Watson. You look very 'Hawaii girl on a date.' I like it." Connor pressed a handful of her wig's long black tresses to his nose. "Even smells real. Will you keep it on for me…later?" He wiggled his brows.

"Ha. We need to talk."

"Women. Always with the talking." His chuckle was strained.

"Not really a joking matter, Connor. We can go to my hostel."

He fell in step with her and they walked the couple of blocks through the warm, plumeria-scented night, holding hands, blending perfectly in the casual beach town atmosphere. Connor stowed his surfboard outside the room's door, and once in her unit, he unzipped a waterproof fanny pack to show a change of clothes—and the Walther PPK he favored. "I'll shower and change, if you don't mind."

"Please do. I'll fix some tea." There was nothing else to eat or drink in the bare space.

Sophie had the tea ready in a pair of paper cups when Connor came out, toweling his short blond hair. She enjoyed the way he moved in the lightweight, upscale trousers he wore with a silk polo shirt that showcased his muscular torso. The fact that he'd come in from the ocean with those clothes to change into —*so James Bond it was ridiculous.*

Connor sat beside her on the bed since there was no other furniture, and took the tea. "Thanks. Can't help wishing this was something stronger." They sipped. "So. You wanted to talk." He patted the bed. "I have something else in mind."

Sophie smiled, his words igniting a warmth that sang along her nerve endings in spite of everything. She had to focus to remember their difficult conversation, his agitation, the uncomfortable questions from Lei and Pono. "You're wrong about Jake and me, and our relationship. He's my partner. Nothing more."

Connor's sea-blue eyes were intent as he toyed with the realistic-looking scruff on his cheeks. "I'd still like to move one of you off-site."

"I'm off-site. And not interested in him, as you have occasion to know." She scooted closer. Their knees brushed. "Don't tarnish my good opinion of you with petty jealousy. It doesn't become you."

"No, it doesn't. I know that, and I can't seem to help myself." He leaned toward her. Their shoulders touched. The hairs on her arms lifted and her nipples tightened. "I don't feel entirely in control around you. And that troubles me," he whispered into her ear, sending a shiver down her spine.

"I know it does. Marcella would call you a control freak." Sophie moved away from his magnetic pull by standing. She paced. "We have to talk about the Ghost."

"Damn it." Connor leaned back on the bed against the pillows, crossing his arms behind his head. His body filled the bed, radiating unsettling power. "Whatever they told you—it's a lie."

"Tell me what's going on. How did they link the Ghost with this agent's death?"

"I'm looking into that and I smell a rat—someone fed intel to the Bureau, setting me up. The Ghost didn't target that agent. There are plenty of other bad fish to fry without tackling any in the Bureau. Until you came across the Ghost's existence on that case last year, no one was aware of its activities."

"It's strange that you talk about yourself in the third person." Sophie put her hands on her hips. "I hope you know that."

"That's how the Ghost is. Separate, in its own little black box. A necessary evil for good."

"That is only a coping mechanism for justifying what it is that the Ghost does. What *you* do." Sophie's breath came fast, anger flushing her body and tightening her muscles. "Deny it however you like—you kill people."

"But I don't. I provide information to evil people and they do what they do to each other. Very different from pulling a trigger."

"But *you* are judge and jury, deciding who knows what, manipulating these people. And now the Bureau is on to you. They've got something on you, and it could put you away forever."

"You say that like you care."

"Of course, I care! *Son of a two-headed poxy goat*! Way more than I ever wanted to!" Sophie's hands balled into fists. "You're endangering *us*!"

"What I am and what I've done as the Ghost was in play long before I met you. Even if I'd stopped the day we got together, it wouldn't make a difference from all that went before." Connor's eyes were dusky blue in the low light.

"It would make a difference to *me*." Sophie's eyes prickled with tears she blinked away. "I want to know you care enough to listen to me."

"I care, Sophie Smithson Ang." Connor's gaze met hers. "Since you're asking me to, I'll give up the Ghost." He smiled a little, and she did too, recognizing the turn of phrase. "I'll give up my mission because you're asking me to. Because you're worth every risk, every price that it'll take to be with you." His voice whispered across her skin, melting her. That streak of darkness in him, so implacable and defiant, was compelling. *The danger of him was sexy.* That he'd put aside his vigilantism for her weakened her knees. "Now, you just have to take a leap of faith and believe me when I tell you I had nothing to do with that agent's death. I'm very careful about what I do. The Ghost makes sure those who get what's coming to them really deserve it. What concerns me about the death of this agent is that he *is* the kind of target I would choose if the Ghost went after someone in the Bureau. He was dirty. Which means someone else knows about me. I have to ask— did you tell anyone?" Connor's eyes looked bruised and vulnerable for the first time. "Because if you have to trust me, I am also trusting you."

Sophie sat down on the edge of the bed. "No. No one. Not even my closest friends. And I've been tempted."

He sat forward and hooked a hand around the back of her neck. "Tempted. Ah, I'm familiar with that feeling." His mouth claimed hers.

Sophie fell across his body and into his arms with a tiny muffled sound of need.

She couldn't get to his skin fast enough, nor he to hers. The sex was rough and hard and over too quickly. But not the next time. Or the time after that.

Chapter Eight

The next day, Dr. Kinoshita smoothed the tailored sheath dress that was her trademark outfit and tucked a wisp of black hair behind her ear. She opened a file at the table in the guest cottage of Miller's estate. Seated around her in the cramped space were Sophie, Jake, Jesse, and Ronnie. "Security Solutions' Vice President Bix and I pulled together all the evidence and information you've gathered on Shank Miller's stalker identifying herself, or perhaps himself, as 'Blondie.' I spent the weekend working on a report to share with you." She distributed copies to each of them. "The first part is just a summary of the information I've gathered. Skim through and check for accuracy, please."

Sophie ran her eyes and a finger down the series of dates identifying when and where contact from Blondie had been made, the type of contact, and other very specific information to the case. After a few minor corrections, mostly from Jake who held the main case file open in front of him, they moved on to the meat of the report.

"I believe this unsub, to borrow from FBI terminology, is a female," Dr. Kinoshita stated.

"I think that would be obvious, what with all the bridal activity and whatnot?" Ronnie raised his brows in question.

"No." Kinoshita's voice was measured. "Stalkers can disguise themselves in different ways, including gender. The sentiments expressed by the stalker may or may not be genuine to his or her real agenda. What convinces me more than anything is forensic evidence in the underwear tossed at Miller during concerts in the initial overtures put forth by the subject. Our lab at Security Solutions identified it as vaginal secretions from the same donor." She took a sip of the coffee Jesse had fetched her. "So, let's get into the meat of things. I see an escalation in the pattern of attacks. And you might say that 'attacks' is too strong a word to use to describe these overtures. But attacks they are, because Blondie is deliberately trying to unsettle and impinge upon our client with her increasingly urgent fantasy of marrying him." Kinoshita ran a finger down to the bottom of the last page. "I gave the stalker a tentative diagnosis of obsessive-compulsive disorder with psychotic features. It's an unusual diagnosis, but I believe it describes both the level of compulsion and lack of reality testing that this subject demonstrates."

"Reality testing?" Jake leaned forward. Dressed in his usual all black, he radiated tension.

"Reality testing is a clinical term for how grounded a subject is in the demonstrable reality of here and now, time and space. We test this in a subject interview by asking about history, current and past time, and perceptions of concrete items. Of course, I can't do that with this subject, but the persistence of the subject's fantasy and the driving quality it has are pathological distortions."

"That seems kind of obvious," Ronnie said. Jake scowled at the young man, but Kinoshita inclined her head in his direction and answered deliberately.

"Every commonsense assumption is not necessarily accurate. It behooves us to examine all possible scenarios, and that is what my job entails. For instance, we've had cases where an apparent malicious stalker has been a business partner with an ax to grind."

"We have focused on a bed partner or a disgruntled girl-friend. And there have been many of those." Jake inclined his head. "Please do give us all that you have."

Kinoshita handed Jake an open file. Jake frowned. "Shank's getting home soon. I'll talk with him about this as soon as possible."

"But what scenario is the most likely, in your view?" Sophie asked. She felt muzzy-headed from so little sleep in spite of two cups of strong tea, her body sensitive and sated but her emotions raw after Connor's departure early in the morning. She planned to join him on Oahu after checking out the lead she had on Assan at the Paradise Treasures Gallery.

"A profile I would put on this subject is the following: female, in her mid-thirties to forties, a person who lives alone and feeds herself on fantasy-based content and entertainment-oriented television. She's following a classic stalker pattern of escalation and she's getting closer to making an attempt to reach Miller in person. When is Miller due back to this location?"

Jake frowned. "He's supposed to be back from Quebec day after tomorrow. He was going to take a few weeks off here on Maui."

"You might consider advising him to take his vacation in another location. Unknown. Keep him off the grid. Perhaps then you can set a trap for Blondie here at the compound. Enlist a confederate who dresses as Miller, and try to lure Blondie out of the shadows."

Sophie suppressed a smile at the enthusiastic glint that lit Jake's eyes at this idea. *Her partner would always rather go on the offensive.* Sitting back inside the walls of the compound and trying to anticipate Blondie's moves rather than going after the stalker in an active way had been driving Jake crazy.

"I think we just got a new project!" Jake rubbed his hands

together. He looked around the table at each member of their little team. "What do you think? All in favor, say 'aye'!"

Sophie, Ronnie, and Jesse echoed his enthusiastic agreement.

Kinoshita smiled. "And I'll really make your day by telling you that Bix has already approved this course of action—with all possible safety protocols in place, of course."

Jake stood up, waving the report. "I want to call Shank and read the pertinent parts of this to him. Get him to change his plans."

"Sounds like you have a plan. I don't see the purpose for me to stay on here with this case at the moment," Sophie said. "My focus is the AI software. If Miller isn't coming back right away, I should return to Oahu. I have a dog that needs me." *And a boyfriend who wants me.*

Jake slowly sat down. "No. You should stay."

"For what?" Sophie lifted her brows.

"Quite frankly, I think you'll be safer here at the compound than anywhere else."

"About that." Kinoshita gazed at Sophie. "Bix and I conferred. In light of your recent attack, we both think it's possible your ex might be hiding here on Maui. If that is the case, contrary to what Jake says, you'd be better off returning to Oahu and taking whatever security measures you deem fit. You'll also be in a better position to work with the FBI on his capture from Honolulu."

"We agree, then. Jake, I wish you luck with this next phase." Sophie stood. "Now if you'll excuse me, I have a few loose ends to tie up before I return to Oahu."

Like checking out the lead on Assan at Paradise Treasures Gallery.

———

SOPHIE WAS HEADING BACK to her new rental car, Mary Watson's sundress fluttering against her legs, when Jake approached, striding toward her from the security cottage. "You weren't even going to say goodbye?"

Sophie rolled her shoulders back, irritated. "Goodbye. I'll see you when either Shank Miller is back on Maui, or you are back on Oahu at the end of this job."

"You're up to something. Tell me what it is."

"Goodbye, Jake. I'll be in touch," Sophie said firmly. She got into the lime green Dodge Neon rental and slammed the door. She pulled out of the compound, adjusting her rearview mirror. Jake seemed to fill the driveway, watching her go, his hands on his hips.

Sophie firmed her jaw.

This was none of his business, and she'd handle it herself. She couldn't endanger either Connor or Jake by attracting Assan's attention to them. She'd learned the hard way with a previous relationship that Assan would go after any man she cared about.

Her mind flashed back to the early morning hours as she lay naked on her side in the small, lumpy bed at the hostel in Paia, the sheet bunched at her waist, a hand propping up her chin as she watched Connor dress. She enjoyed the warm caress of lamplight over his tanned chest and chiseled abs as he pulled up the tailored slacks and zipped them, threaded a belt through the loops, and reached for the shirt she'd just about torn off him hours before. "Did you find out anything new about your ex?"

"No," she lied. "Are you going to tell me the lead you have on him?"

"It's this. He's on Maui." Connor's hands stilled on the buttons of his shirt as his eyes, lit by shadows, found hers. "All the more reason for you to come back to Oahu. Now tell me what you know."

"No."

Connor stopped buttoning the shirt and came over to the bed. Just his closeness made her soften with longing, but Sophie held her position, refusing to move as he leaned over her, smelling of soap and man and all the ecstasy they'd experienced. "This is so dysfunctional," he whispered into her mouth. "I can't wait until it's over."

"Will it ever be over?" She breathed him in, her eyes fluttering shut.

"I hope not." His mouth closed the distance to meet hers.

Sophie put a hand up to touch her lips, still tingling at the memory. *Dysfunctional, for sure, but irresistible.*

She could worry about where things were going with Connor when Assan was in custody.

Chapter Nine

H is wife had taken the bait.

Facial recognition software, loaded on the gallery's security cameras, picked up Sophie, even with the hat and sunglasses she wore into the place. Assan watched her on a phone surveillance app, his eyes avid for any glimpse of her face, any betraying gesture. The spotlights of the gallery skimmed over her skin so that she appeared to emerge and then vanish in the grainy feed. He couldn't see her face, though, hidden as it was by the shadow of her hat, and his hands balled into fists.

Sophie was dressed differently. The camera picked up the solid shape of her toned shoulders, the firm rounds of her butt. He liked how feminine she looked; the floral dress she wore with sandals flattered her fit, beautiful body. She was still strong enough to put up a fight, and that flushed him with heat.

Assan texted his men even as he continued to watch what silently unfolded. He'd lost track of her after that first, botched kidnap attempt, but he wouldn't make that mistake again.

Sophie approached the gallery's owner, Magda Kennedy. He and Kennedy had come to an understanding. He was a silent partner, providing cash flow during an uncomfortable crunch. In return, he was staying at lodgings she owned, no questions asked, no details given. She had agreed to the extra security measures that allowed him to watch Sophie as the two women talked, surrounded by stunning artworks, and finally Kennedy led Sophie over to a painting, spotlighted by a harsh beam of light.

She must have some very good trolling program to pick up the crumbs he dropped for her, crumbs too subtle, too personal for the FBI or Interpol—but he'd counted on her being able to find them.

His palms sweat with desire as he watched her.

A smile tugged up his lips as Assan anticipated how ruined she'd be by what he had planned for her next—it would soften her up for when he got his hands on her.

―――――

"I'M SHOPPING for my home collection and I would like something with an Asian feeling. I spent some time in Hong Kong in the past. Do you have anything that ties to that area?" Sophie asked, fiddling with her purse strap. This role as a wealthy art-collecting woman didn't feel natural, but she'd tried to at least look the part, wearing a pair of huge natural pearls given to her by her father, and an upscale sundress.

Magda Kennedy's crystal blue eyes contrasted with jet-black hair and brows as finely marked as calligraphy. The stunning woman wore a white, off the shoulder Grecian-style dress and gold, kitten-heeled sandals with cords wrapping her calves. She looked as if she'd just walked down from Olympus to sell art in Lahaina.

Her dark brows scrunched delicately. "I don't have anything from there specifically, but I have an Asian collection I'll show you." Kennedy led Sophie toward the back of the gallery. Sophie tried not to swing her head or give any other indication that she was taking in all the information that she could about the gallery and its owner. "This is a beautiful gallery in a prime location. You must do a high volume."

"It's a bit seasonal. I'm not out on the floor except during our peak times." Kennedy spoke coolly over her shoulder.

"I've always wanted to invest in an art gallery." Sophie let her sentence trail off, hoping Kennedy might volunteer something. Once again, she was aware of her limitations as a field operative. Her friend Marcella was so much more glib, easily able to interview a witness without seeming to. Truth was, Sophie had no idea how to find out if Assan was involved with this gallery, other than hacking the woman's computers, which she'd already done. She'd found nothing of interest other than a shortage of cash flow being propped up temporarily by a business loan from an unknown investor. *Could that investor be Assan?*

"Many people imagine being involved with the art world," Kennedy said neutrally. "It's almost as common a fantasy as writing a book."

Sophie struggled for another leading question. "Do you store all your art on-site?" At least she could find out if there was more of the gallery she could investigate, and look for indicators of Assan's presence.

Kennedy stopped suddenly, and Sophie almost bumped into her. "Are you interested in a piece of art, or not?"

Heat flashed on Sophie's cheekbones. "Of course." She drew herself taller, clipping her words in a haughty manner. "I was just making conversation. I'm happy to take my business elsewhere, if my questions make you uncomfortable."

"My mistake." Kennedy turned away. "I think you'll appreciate this unique piece I'd like to show you."

The woman was now suspicious, so Sophie ended up paying way too much for an antique Chinese watercolor. She left it at the gallery to be professionally framed because that would provide an excuse to return.

Sophie shook Kennedy's hand at the door. "Thank you for a lovely art piece that I will enjoy for many years."

"And mahalo to you for coming in today." Kennedy had definitely warmed up at the pile of cash Mary Watson had produced to pay for the art piece.

Sophie would have to get more money before she went back to Oahu. Mary Watson's bank account was periodically filled by Sophie's trust fund, routed through a couple of shell corporations she had set up. She used it as little as possible, because it could provide a link to her if a searcher was careful enough to find it. She hadn't yet figured out how to obtain an untraceable stream of cash to live on as Mary Watson.

Sophie thought about that as she walked out, conscious of a feeling of being watched.

She was beginning to get used to that feeling, a tightness between her shoulder blades as if a finger rested there.

Chapter Ten

Sophie's burner phone rang on the seat of the rental car as she drove back toward Paia, and she spotted Jake's number. She pulled over to answer it at a tiny turnout on the Pali, that winding and dramatic cliff route from the main town of Kahului to Lahaina on the western side of the island. Cobalt ocean foamed around black volcanic rocks thousands of feet below, and Sophie's gaze feasted on the purple-brown smudge of the tiny barrier island of Kahoolawe, resting like smoke on the horizon. "Hello, Jake."

"Are you still on island? Because I need you to come back to the compound." Jake said.

"Why?" Sophie frowned. A strong gust of wind batted at the little car.

"Shank is on a plane to Maui from Canada. He got some of those dolls delivered to his hotel in Quebec, and he's spooked. Refuses to go elsewhere to hide; says he's coming home to Maui for a badly needed vacation, and that we can use him for bait to flush Blondie out."

"Afterbirth of conjoined twins!"

"Whatever you just said is my feeling exactly. I called Bix

and he agrees you should come back to the house. Help me manage our rock star and the situation. I've already worked with the guys on an op to capture Blondie; we've got extra security cams and stuff to set up that I'd like to run by you. I really need you here."

Sophie sighed. "All right. But I won't stay long."

"We can argue about that later. For now, get your ass back here."

"Do not talk to me like I am one of your men to be ordered about," Sophie snapped.

"Sorry. I just…" Sophie could practically see Jake pushing a hand through his hair in annoyance. "Just come back here so we can go over the plan, please. *Partner.* Equal. Most ass-kicking female of my acquaintance whose expertise I need on this case."

"That's better." She smiled. "On my way."

————

SHANK MILLER LOOKED EVEN PALER than Sophie remembered as one of his bodyguards opened the limo's door. Decorative chains clanked from his leathers as he got out, his long hair bundled back and rings gleaming in his ears. The man likely slept during the day to rest up for his nighttime concerts, much like the vampire he resembled.

Sophie had changed out of Mary Watson's outfit in the guest room into her standard work outfit, and she stood with the other staff as the rocker greeted Jake with a hug and backslap. Antigua, Pepe, and their two junior security staff all stood in a row with Sophie on the end, a queue of servants greeting the lord of the manor upon his return.

Miller worked his way down the line of staff, greeting them and asking personal questions about their family and health. *No wonder the man was popular.*

"Hello, beautiful," Miller purred when he reached Sophie, taking her hand to press a kiss on the back of it. His dark eyes, lined in kohl, twinkled up at her. "I have been working out hard. Trying to build some bulk."

"That's nice, Mr. Miller. I'm sure your health has benefited," Sophie said politely. Clearly the rocker had not forgotten an earlier, tactless comment she had made about his physique. "I would be happy to join you for a workout some time."

"I will take you up on that. So, remind me of your role here, again?" He hadn't let go of Sophie's hand, and Jake frowned from behind the rocker's back.

"I'm Jake's partner with Security Solutions. My specialty is computers and I'm here to support your team, but mostly to train the artificial intelligence home monitoring security system we've installed," Sophie said.

Miller turned to Jake. "Brilliant *and* beautiful."

"I know. And you're only schmoozing her because she said you look like a heroin addict and implied you weren't attractive."

"I was struck to the heart," Miller agreed. "My delicate male ego is still trying to recover."

Sophie removed her hand from Miller's and rubbed residual dampness on her pants, a gesture he watched with fascination. "Like I said, I'll be pleased to work out with you some time. I hope you are not still offended."

"Is she always this literal?" Miller asked Jake.

"Afraid so." They both studied her.

Sophie cleared her throat. "We should really move on to more urgent business, like the problem of Blondie and how to catch her. You should be flattered, Mr. Miller. Some women would like to love you to death. Literally."

"Don't remind me." Miller shook his head and turned to head for the double doors of the mansion, addressing the two bodyguards standing by the limo. "Butch, Andy, bring my things and that nastiness that was delivered to my hotel room. I'll meet you all in the living room once I've had a shower and feel human again from the plane flight."

———

WHEN THE SECURITY SOLUTIONS team gathered, sitting around an octagonal card table to review the Blondie situation, Shank did look better. Sipping a green drink Antigua had prepared for him, he gestured to the bag of Barbie dolls on the table. "I want to know how Blondie found me in Quebec. As you can see, I gave Butch and Andy the night off so we could speak freely." He took another sip of the green drink. "Herold, my bodyguard for the longest amount of time, retired last year and I just don't trust these two the same way. Can you check them out? I mean, more thoroughly than just the usual background check?" Miller's eyes found Sophie. "I hear you have some sort of super program that can find out everything about a guy down to his dick size."

"That would be an unusual search parameter," Sophie said, as Jesse and Ronnie snorted with laughter. "But yes, I can do a deeper background check on them, pull up their financials and so on—though I must warn you, it's not strictly legal to do so."

Miller waved a hand. "They've signed agreements to have transparent records, not that I've utilized that clause in the contract. No one but my immediate team knew my location in Quebec, and I went in and out of the hotel in disguise. I'm worried one of them sold me out."

Jake sat forward, resting his elbows on the green felt surface of the table. "We discussed how Blondie got dolls into the estate here while you were gone, which seemed to show she didn't know where you were. It's concerning to see that she found you."

"That's why I'm home now." Miller drained the last of the health drink.

Sophie picked up the bag to examine three new plastic figures. "Any prints on these?"

"No. The guys checked," Miller said.

Sophie shook the figures out onto the card table and examined them closely. Each one was labeled with a day and time of retrieval. The blonde female figures continued to wear bridal outfits, but the mutilations on the male figure had progressed: both arms missing, both arms and a leg, and finally, limbless and sawed in half.

The attention to detail on the hand-drawn tattoos was remarkable.

"That last one sure is creepy." Miller pointed to the dismembered doll, his mouth twisted down.

"Indeed it is." Sophie looked up at Jake. "Did you tell Mr. Miller what Dr. Kinoshita said in her evaluation?"

"Female. Obsessed. Escalating. There's a potential for bodily harm if she gets ahold of you," Jake told Miller.

The rocker shuddered. "God forbid."

"You should read the report." Jake pushed a copy from his file over to Miller.

Miller pushed it back. "I'm having enough trouble sleeping without giving this psycho any more room in my head. I trust you all to handle this." He stood abruptly. "I'm going to get some rest. Let me know when you've come up with a plan to catch this bitch." He left, and closed the door a little too hard.

Sophie looked at Jake and their two staffers. "He seems upset."

"Wouldn't you be? Look into the backgrounds of those bodyguards, pronto. I ran the usual Security Solutions protocol on them and found nothing."

"I will, of course." Sophie frowned thoughtfully, picking up one of the dolls. "I don't remember seeing this 'tattoo' drawn on one of these dolls before." Sophie pointed to a tattoo on the male figure's groin, an area beneath what would have been his beltline and not visible to public scrutiny. "Looks like it might have been someone Miller had sex with? I don't believe there are photos circulating of this tattoo, do you?"

"We've thought of that. Have a whole album of blondes he's slept with, and mini-profiles on them," Jake said. "I can show them to you, if you like. Shank is partial to blondes, so there've been a lot."

"Not necessary right now. This person really studied his tattoos. Have you considered it might be one of the artists who worked on him?"

Jake's brows snapped together in a frown. "No. But that's a good lead to pursue. In the meantime, I want to lay out our ideas to lure Blondie out into the open. And until we clear his bodyguards and the rest of the staff, the plan doesn't go beyond this room."

Chapter Eleven

Done with the meeting eventually, Sophie dove into the familiar wired world as soon as she'd set up her laptop in the same guest room she'd used before. Putting on her headphones, turning up the air conditioning, dimming the lights, she settled her body into an ergonomic chair as her fingers flew over the keyboard. *Not even sleeping felt so much like an escape.*

She had missed the gray maze of the cyber world, a place where she traveled weightless, bodiless, fast and free, screened from distractions by Beethoven crashing in her ears.

Sophie routed the cams set around the house into the central processing software and sped up the image integration, gathering all the bits and pieces gathered over the time that Security Solutions had been working at Miller's house. She then launched the compilation and assessment algorithm and trained the cameras on Miller's sleeping and living areas. A few days of data gathering, and the AI software would have all the information it needed, now that the master of the house was back in residence.

She moved on to using DAVID for a deep background check on the two bodyguards. It didn't take long to uncover a financial weakness in the profile of Daniel "Butch" Callahan, the older of the guards. A former Army sergeant, Callahan was in debt to two ex-wives and seemed to have a gambling problem, if his frequent flights to Vegas were any indication. He ran a balance close to redline in most of his accounts.

A touch on her shoulder jerked Sophie around. She took off her headphones. "Antigua! I'm sorry, I didn't hear you come in."

Antigua set a tray heaped with beautiful island food onto the desk beside Sophie. "Half of a sunrise papaya, filled with home-made yogurt. Pineapple muffin. Mango pancakes." She set a large mug of steaming, dark liquid beside it. "And Thai tea, just the way you like it."

Sophie pushed her chair back from the desk, reaching up to stretch her arms above her head, groaning at the stiffness. "You are very kind, Antigua. Thank you."

Antigua squeezed Sophie's shoulder. "I don't know if you noticed, but it's two p.m."

"I got absorbed in my work." Sophie shook her head, but that made her aware of the beginnings of a headache behind her eyes, tired from focusing on the screen. "I lost track of time." She picked up the tea and took a sip. "This is delicious."

"I have to keep our best computer gal fueled up." Antigua rested a hip on the desk as Sophie sat down and dug into the papaya, moaning at the delicious taste and sensuous texture. "We've been worried about you since the attack on the beach."

"Jake is a …" Sophie search for the word, trying out an Americanism. "Fussbudget."

"Not just Jake. Our whole team has been concerned." Antigua straightened the linen napkin she had brought with the meal, smoothing the seams precisely beside Sophie's plate. "I hope you're okay. I have been sending you positive energy."

"Thank you. Knowing that my ex is loose and trying to kill me is difficult." Sophie looked up at the other woman. "It's good to be back at my computer, to have something to take my mind off it."

"I understand." Antigua paused for a moment. She cast her eyes down and cleared her throat. "Jake and I are sleeping together. I just thought you should know."

Sophie's face froze into the neutral mask she had learned to hide behind. Her chest seized up but she made herself breathe normally. *She didn't care, did she?* She'd made choices, and so had Jake.

"None of my business. I already have a boyfriend." Sophie's heart pounded with strange, slow thumps as if a hand were squeezing it. "But I'd think my partner would have told me if he wanted me to know something so personal."

"You know guys." Antigua flipped a hand and smiled, her luminous teeth flashing. "The last to kiss and tell." She stood with a fluid movement. "But you're partners, so I thought I'd keep you in the loop. I think he was really into you at one time. I hope you're okay with the situation. Wouldn't want it to be awkward."

"Why would it be awkward?" Sophie made herself smile. "I'm glad for Jake to have someone. Just like I do."

"We're having fun." Antigua's smile was so bright it hurt Sophie's eyes. *She really liked Jake.* "I'll let him know I told you."

The woman squeezed Sophie's shoulder again as she left the room, leaving the scent of Tahitian gardenias in her wake.

Sophie had the same feeling as when that Welsh fighter Mega Hammer had caught her in the solar plexus last year and her breath had been blasted out of her lungs. She forced herself to finish the food on the plate. *That assessing look in Antigua's eyes had been measuring how attached Sophie was to Jake.*

No, it was none of Sophie's business what those two did in their private time. She had chosen Connor, and just thinking about their night together warmed her, in spite of all the questions that remained.

Done with the meal in spite of her lack of appetite, Sophie took the plate into the kitchen and rinsed the dishes at the sink, relieved Antigua was nowhere to be seen.

Jake entered, dressed in his usual all-black, vibrating with energy. "Did you make any progress?"

"I did." Just looking at him, Sophie felt better. She really was glad he had someone—*he deserved to be loved!* "Looks like there might be an issue with one of the...subjects." Sophie flicked her head in the direction of the camera embedded in the corner of the kitchen. Talking about the bodyguards on video was not a good idea. Jake gave a curt nod.

"Let's go to the surveillance center and you can get me up to speed."

He led her toward the guest cottage where the center was set up. The main room was cluttered with surveillance equipment, monitors, and the personal items of three men living in close quarters, and Sophie immediately felt claustrophobic, glad to have her own bedroom and workstation elsewhere in the house. She perched on a seat at the small multipurpose round table. "Did you talk to Detective Cruz about what happened to Miller in Quebec? What is MPD doing to address the increased threat?"

"I did call Cruz, and he said they'd try to throw a few more patrols our way. Cruz said that there's really not much they can do. Certainly not more than we can do as a professional team on the premises. But let me get you up to speed on some leads we have, and I'll give you the final psych report to read." Jake unlocked a metal cabinet and withdrew a file. "For you to take back to your room. Dr. Kinoshita wants hard copy only, as a security measure—this report should not get circulated."

"Of course." Sophie took the file as Jake lifted a magnetized felt cover off of a hidden white board on the wall. Various theories were brainstormed off of a cartoon drawing of Shank. *Ex-Girlfriend or Sex Partner* was the biggest offshoot, with names and dates branching off of the topic. Additional categories included *Former Employee, Concert groupie/Fan, Someone from Early Life.* A small new branch, dated today in a different color, was labeled *Tattoo Artist Connection?*

"This reminds me of my FBI days." Sophie said. "This is more than a standard security firm would do."

"Of course. If we find the perp, we'll provide the best security for our client, especially given the constraints of local law enforcement." Jake said. "Besides, we're Security Solutions, not some cheesy rent-a-cop outfit."

"Yes." Sophie looked down at the folder in front of her. "Well, I have some reading here to do. But as for the bodyguards, I think we should warn Miller that Butch Callahan has a debt issue and is vulnerable—though I didn't see any payments coming in to deal with his current debt load. Likely he'd try to conceal that." She filled Jake in on what DAVID had uncovered. "Did you decide when we're going to try to capture Blondie?"

"Tomorrow night. You're to stay inside the compound and monitor via electronic security." His statement was terse and flat.

"I heard the plan in the den." Sophie suppressed a wave of irritation. *He was always trying to bully her into a passive role.* "As soon as it's executed, I'll be leaving. Anything else?"

Jake turned away from the board, an abrupt movement. His biceps bulged as he jammed the lid onto his pen with unnecessary force, his face stoic. "No, nothing. Since you're in such a hurry to be on your way."

Sophie felt an answering flare of anger, a hot coal that melted some of the chill around her heart. "I don't know what you want from me."

"Something you've never been willing to give."

Sophie's nostrils flared. "You're sleeping with Antigua, and you're acting like I owe you something?" She stood up, smacking the folder down on the table like a rifle shot. *"Son of a poxy whore!"*

Jake's eyes widened. "Cuss me out in English, if you're going to insult me. I just meant friendship. Honesty. You're always shutting me out, and I don't know why."

"Because I don't *like* you, Jake Dunn. You're a loud, type

A, annoying alpha male who's always getting in my space, both physically and emotionally, and trying to bully and protect me when I don't need it." Sophie's pulse hammered in her veins and her hands had drawn into fists. "How's that for honesty?"

Jake waited a beat. "Antigua must have told you we were banging. Are you jealous?" He cocked his head. "Is that why you're so pissed off?"

"*Banging?* That's your word for it? Oh, my God." Sophie slammed back the chair and headed for the door. *"Preening peacock! Foul breath of an infidel!* You're disgusting!"

"Sorry for irritating you with my personal life," Jake called after her as Sophie slammed the door of the cottage.

She strode back to her room.

Was she jealous? *No!* She was infuriated by Jake's demeaning attitude toward Antigua—a capable, skilled, beautiful woman who deserved more, probably hoped for more, and was going to get her heart broken.

Sophie was too agitated to read the psychologist's report. She changed into exercise clothes and went to the state-of-the-art gym off the back of the house.

Shank Miller was sitting on a reclining bike, pedaling in a desultory way, doodling on a pad of paper. Headphones cradled long hair pulled back in a ponytail. His narrow, tattooed white torso was eerily familiar to Sophie because of the montage of skin art she'd memorized through examining the plastic figures —but a buff, tan Ken doll he was not. At the sight of her, Miller sped up and set the notebook aside.

Sophie picked up a weighted jump rope from a neat stack of gear on a shelf in one corner of the room. "If you are looking for bulk, the bike probably isn't the best choice."

"I need stamina just as much," Miller said. "I burn a lot of calories during a concert, and I need to keep my energy up for several hours at a time."

"Well then, disregard. I'm sure Jake has taken everything

you need in your routine into consideration." Sophie found a spot on the padded mat and began jumping, warming up.

"Jake was in Special Forces. Imagine those guys faced every kind of threat." Miller resumed pedaling, and for a while they worked out in companionable silence, the slap of Sophie's weighted rope a counterpoint to the smooth whirring of Miller's machine.

After twenty minutes, Sophie's muscles were sufficiently warmed up and she switched to her free weight routine. Miller got off the bike and lay down on the bench press. He had too much weight on his bar, but Sophie didn't comment until the rocker was stuck, pinned beneath and struggling to lift it.

She walked over behind his head and hefted the bar back into the cradle. "I'm sure it's hard to keep up with your workouts when you're on the road. You should ease into it now that you're home for a while."

Miller sat up, mopping his face with a towel. "I feel like I have to do everything I can, considering what's going on with the stalker."

"That's what you have our team for," Sophie said. "Jake and the men have everything under control. And I will have an open line to law enforcement throughout tomorrow night's operation."

Miller's dark eyes were intent. "Do you think this is the right way to go about things? Trying to flush Blondie out?"

"Jake is in charge of your security. I have a limited role," Sophie hedged. She leaned over and picked up a twenty-pound kettlebell. "I'm just the tech support."

"That tells me you aren't really confident in this operation."

"Not at all." Sophie did a dead lift with the weight, feeling the strain through her back, hips, glutes, and the back of her legs. "I'm just a little more conservative than Jake. But aren't you sick of waiting to see what the stalker will do next? I know your team is, and flushing the unsub out into the open will at least try to bring things to a head."

Miller watched Sophie lift with an appreciative gleam in his eye. "You dating anybody?"

Sophie set the weight down. "As a matter of fact, I am."

Miller sighed, and resumed lifting the barbell Sophie had lightened. "All the good ones are already taken."

She couldn't think of how to respond, so kept silent.

"Has Jake shown you any self-defense moves?" Sophie eventually asked.

"He has, but I'm a little rusty. Butch and Andy were after me to practice while we were on tour, but I just didn't have the energy."

"There is an American phrase for that: 'putting your head in the sand.' I'm not sure what the phrase relates to, exactly, but it seems to mean that you're ignoring something, hoping it will go away. The stalker is not going away, and you might need to defend yourself. I have reason to know. I was attacked just off of your estate, on the beach."

Miller sat up in alarm. "No one told me. Was it related to my case?"

"We don't think so. Turns out I have my own enemies." Sophie's mouth felt tight with suppressed anger and pain. "Come practice some moves with me. It will be good for both of us to have a little refresher."

Miller got off the weight bench quickly and joined Sophie in the small padded sparring ring set up in the middle of the workout area.

They reviewed holds and ways to break them. Miller was attempting to gouge Sophie's eyes with his thumbs when Jake came in. "Giving our boy a self-defense skills review?"

"Indeed, I was." Sophie stepped back from Miller and dropped her arms. "But now that you're here, you can take over."

"Hey!" Miller tried to follow Sophie out through the padded ropes defining the space. "We were just getting started!"

"And that's why we should continue," Jake said smoothly,

sliding into the ring past her. He winked at Sophie, an acknowl-edgment of their mutual role in motivating and protecting Miller.

Sophie was still annoyed with him, and turned away. "I will see you gentlemen later."

Sophie's phone rang as she was heading back to her quarters. "Hey, Sophie! I'm off in a few minutes and Stevens is home with the baby. Want to meet for a drink and some live music?" Lei's voice was upbeat, and Sophie's spirits rose immediately.

"That would be excellent. I need to get out of this testosterone-filled area."

Lei laughed. "Getting sick of the man-splaining, eh? Meet me at the Tiki Lounge in Kihei in twenty minutes. Wear something pretty."

————

WAILEA WAS beautiful at any time of day, and early evening was no exception. Driving through manicured, winding streets beneath arching shade trees on her way to the nearby town of Kihei, Sophie mulled over her reaction to Antigua's news and her argument with Jake. Her mind returned to the hours spent in Paia with Connor, to their passion and closeness. For better or for worse, their relationship was progressing.

Was she doing the right thing, being with him? Not just the right thing for her body—but the right thing for her heart, emotions, and career? Having to hold secrets from her friends caused a tightness in Sophie's chest that never really went away, even though he'd promised to give up his activities.

She pulled into the South Shore Tiki Lounge, a kitschy bar tucked beneath shading bamboo and banyan trees. The sides were open to stands of torch ginger and the outdoors, and Sophie felt right at home weaving among the casual tables past a musician playing slack-key guitar.

Lei was already at the bar, looking slim and pretty in a short black skirt and tank top. A sunrise shell necklace gleamed against her lightly freckled, bronzy skin. She stood when she saw Sophie, holding two drinks: a beer, and Sophie's favorite foamy concoction. "Got you a Blue Hawaiian. Heard this monstrosity is your favorite."

"I love these awful things," Sophie admitted. She took the drink and sipped from the straw. "You must have changed into that outfit. You look very nice."

"No sense going to girls' night out looking like a cop," Lei said, evaluating Sophie's appearance. "I like that girly-girl thing you've got going on, too."

"I have a feminine side." Sophie smoothed the coral-colored halter dress from her alter ego Mary Watson's closet. She liked how the bare back displayed her musculature, and the color set off her tawny brown skin. "I hope this evening's memory will replace the one from the last time I went to a bar for a drink. It ended with me sick on the side of the road, and almost sleeping with Jake."

"Ooh, fate worse than death!" Lei teased. "I remember that debacle. How is Jake?"

They sat at a table in the corner, and took menus from a waiter wearing a hula skirt over his shorts. "He is as usual."

"As usual? What does that mean?" Lei leaned in toward Sophie, squinting. "You look like you're sucking a lemon."

"He is, and I quote, 'banging' Antigua, the lovely chef and property manager at Shank Miller's."

"Hmm." Lei's mouth disappeared into the head of foam on her beer, but it looked like she was smiling.

Sophie frowned. "You are wondering why I care."

"You said it, not me." Lei dabbed at the foam on her lips as the waiter returned. They ordered buffalo wings, mini tacos, and a plate of vegetables that would suffice for dinner.

"What I object to is him trivializing sexual activities with a worthy woman," Sophie said, plucking the umbrella off her drink.

"You like her. And you think he should treat her better."

"That's it exactly." *But that wasn't it exactly.* A niggling bad feeling lingered in Sophie's gut. "It makes me not respect him that he is treating her like that—it disappoints me that he's taking advantage of her. Because she really likes him more than he does her."

"And how do you know that?"

Sophie scowled. "I just know." She shut her eyes to savor a big draft of the sweet, creamy drink. She so seldom allowed herself these indulgences.

"Maybe it's just 'banging' for both of them. They're both sexually liberated single adults, living in a close proximity situation."

"That's all it is for him. But not for her."

"And how is that your problem?" Lei's large brown eyes sparkled. She seemed to be hinting at something, but Sophie was never sure of these social nuances.

"It *isn't* my problem. I already have a boyfriend."

"Ah. So, you've finally graduated to calling him that."

The food arrived, giving Sophie a moment to think through her conflicted feelings. She picked up a spear of sliced raw zucchini and dipped it in hummus on the vegetable platter. "Todd and I are a couple now."

"You're trying to say that like you mean it, but you still aren't sure about him." Lei bit into a buffalo wing and sighed happily. "Been ages since I've had these."

"How do you know I'm not sure about him? I *am* sure about him!" Sophie's voice was too loud and she moderated. "He is an amazing man, one in a million. Statistically, one in a billion is more likely. If that."

"I'm not disagreeing. Todd Remarkian seems like the total package. I just know you, and I can tell you're not sure about him." Lei picked up another piece of chicken. "Kiet would make such a mess if he got his little hands on these wings, with this sauce."

Sophie looked around the bright, busy bar at the other patrons, disturbed by her friend's insight. All she couldn't tell Lei about Connor and his secrets stuck in her throat as if she'd ingested a bone from one of the buffalo wings. *Lei was right.* She wasn't sure about Connor, on a number of levels, and she couldn't tell Lei anything about why. *Time to change the subject.* "How did you know when you and Michael were meant to be together? You seem so happy."

Lei laughed. "I took way too long with that. I'm the last person you should ask for love life advice—we have had a bumpy road, to say the least. But there was just something between us that neither of us could ever give up."

Sophie swallowed the last of her drink and waved at the waiter for another. "I really want Jake to be happy. I don't know why I care what he does, with Antigua or anyone else. I hated how he used to flirt with me."

"Well, do you want me to tell you why you're so twisted up?" Lei had a dimple when she smiled a certain way.

"If you must." Sophie straightened stiffly in her chair and picked up a mini taco for something to do with her hands. "I have a feeling I will not like your opinion."

"See, look at you. Got your back up like a wet cat." Lei set her beer down. "This is my one shot to lay it out as I see it, so here goes. It's obvious you and Jake are attracted to each other, and you've become attached to him in spite of yourself, in spite of how irritating he can be. If you gave yourself half a chance, you'd fall for him like a bag of hammers, and he's already gone on you, which is how you know he isn't really into Antigua. But you've got more baggage than a 747, my friend, and because of it you've hitched your wagon to a guy who will never really be there for you."

A long pause as Sophie made herself take a bite of the taco and chew, trying not to instantly repudiate Lei's words. She wiped her hands on her napkin and frowned. "There were too many metaphors in that speech. And I don't know why you would say that about Todd. He's told me he loves me. And I love him."

Lei shrugged. "Then I'm totally wrong. Forget I ever said anything."

"But you must tell me why you don't think Todd will 'be there' for me. He already was there when I was injured!"

"There's just something about him that's not quite…I don't know. Maybe he's just too perfect, and that's what bothers me." Lei's smile was brilliant. "But don't forget who you're talking to. If you have a 747 worth of personal baggage, mine would fill a cruise ship."

Chapter Twelve

The next night, Sophie sat in the command center, a prickle of perspiration gathering in the groove of her spine as she watched the monitors.

Darkness had dropped a black velvet cloak over the mansion as Miller paced around the perimeter of the estate, giving every indication of restlessness and having difficulty sleeping. He held a small digital tape recorder in one hand, muttering into it, his favorite method of composition. Blondie likely knew that, because Miller had described his process in numerous interviews.

Out of view but positioned nearby outside the compound, Jake and their team waited, hidden amid the shrubbery. When they were setting up earlier, dressing in night camouflage outfits and face paint, the preparations had seemed a little ridiculous— but now, if Sophie hadn't known where they were, she would not have been able to see them.

With a frustrated gesture that looked entirely genuine, Miller scowled at the house and then turned and opened the Plexiglas gate, pushing it open and walking out onto the starlit beach.

Sophie frowned, trying to see, but the range of the surveillance cams was limited.

Her earbud crackled with Jake's voice as she listened in to what was piped into Miller's earpiece. "Keep going, out into the open. Walk back and forth like we discussed, in front of the building. Sophie, call Shank on his cell and direct him to come back."

All these things had been rehearsed. "Roger that." Sophie speed dialed Miller's cell phone.

At the edge of visibility in the grainy feed, Miller picked up, his voice sharp and annoyed. "What? I'm tired of being babysat!"

"That sounds very genuine, Mr. Miller. Give me some verbal abuse, please," Sophie said. "You are known for being stubborn."

"Is that so?" Miller huffed. "If I've told you once, I've told you a million times—I come to Maui to relax and unwind! This shit with all of your security people hovering around is killing my creative mojo. This island is my refuge, and hell if I'll let some obsessed bimbo fan steal it from me!"

"Very good, Mr. Miller. Now move away down the beach to the area we discussed."

Miller shut off the phone without further comment, sliding it into his pocket and stomping off down the beach.

Sophie could no longer see the action as it moved out of video range, so per the plan, she switched on the digital camera installed in Jake's night vision goggles. "Secondary camera on," she said into her headset.

"Roger that." Jake said. His audio piped in too, and she could hear his deep, even breathing. Her partner hadn't even broken a sweat while she got up and stood behind her chair, shifting to ease muscles knotted with tension.

Miller continued his muttering and pacing, walking back and forth in front of the mansion, working his way closer and closer to the tree line, his outline a ghostly green seen through Jake's night vision.

She could tell Miller was tiring by his flagging steps—and finally the rocker sat down, his back to a bank of heavy vegetation fronting the mansion next to his, a mansion Sophie knew too well from her last case.

Jake gave a sudden grunt. Sophie started as her partner lunged up and went on the move.

A pale shadow had detached itself from the bushes and swept toward Miller.

"Move in!" Jake hissed, and the camera went blurry with the power and speed of his movement as he hurtled toward their client and whoever was approaching Miller.

Sophie reached for her own weapon, pulling the Glock as she ran through the house without conscious thought, barreling down the veranda, across the porch, and out through the gate.

A cluster of dark, moving bodies marked the action, and Sophie arrived to see all three of their security team wrestling a white-robed figure. Miller stood back, still on his feet, and Sophie grasped him by an arm. "Come with me." She gave a sharp tug. "We need to get you inside, to a secure location."

Miller resisted, clearly wanting to watch the outcome.

"This is for your own safety, Mr. Miller!" Sophie dealt with his stubbornness by twisting his arm up behind his back. Miller emitted a yelp that reverberated in all of their comms, and Jake spared a quick glance at Sophie and gestured for her to take their client away.

"Damn it!" The rocker struggled and tried one of the restraint breaking moves Sophie had taught him. "I can take care of myself!"

"Please don't act like a child," Sophie snapped. Her harsh words seemed to snap him out of it. Miller stopped struggling, slogging through the sand toward the compound. Sophie let go and followed.

They had almost reached the gate when Sophie was

knocked sideways by a powerful blow. She fell to her knees, fumbling for her weapon.

"Get inside!" Sophie screamed to Miller, who lurched toward the gate. *"Jake!"*

A black shadow hit her like an anvil, and the darkness was complete.

———

SECONDS OR HOURS had passed when Sophie came to—it had been seconds, she decided, because she was flat on her face with sand in her mouth as voices yelled overhead.

"Let us go or I'll blow his head off right here. Drop your weapons! All of you!" A female voice, rough with emotion. *Blondie.*

Jake's voice rumbled nearby, low and reasonable. "Clever to set a diversion like that. I can see that you're serious. But you can understand we can't just let you take Mr. Miller off the premises."

"I won't hurt him if you let us go. We are meant to be together!"

Sophie wiggled her foot—yes. *All reflexes present and accounted for.* She gently pushed the sand out of her mouth with her tongue as she assessed the feet moving past her line of vision: Miller's bare feet in black jeans, and an unknown pair in white athletic shoes.

Sophie shook off the last of the glancing blow that had stunned her. Blondie, a dim white shape, backed past Sophie, holding Miller by the arm with a gun to his head. Jake and their men faced the woman on her other side.

If Sophie could get enough power…

Sophie shoved up onto her hands and knees, swinging a leg around in a powerful sidekick that caught Blondie in the back of the legs.

The woman gave a cry. Her knees buckled just as Miller

shoved an elbow back hard into the woman's solar plexus, stomping on her foot at the same time. He wrenched forward and away in one of the moves they'd so recently practiced.

A blast sucked Sophie's eardrums as the woman's gun fired. Sophie flattened instinctively, sensing the vortex of Jake's movement as he leapt on the woman and bore her to the ground, wrenching the weapon away. He flung Blondie over onto her face in the sand, cuffing her. Keening cries tore from the woman's mouth as she struggled and fought.

Sophie bounded to her feet, weapon drawn. She reached out to pull Miller behind her. "Anyone hurt?"

Ronnie and Jesse, dark shadows holding another restrained figure, responded. "All good here, Ms. Ang."

Jake stood up from restraining the woman. "Her shot went wide, thank God. Let's get these two inside. Ronnie, call the cops."

Ronnie answered in the affirmative, working his phone as Jake unlocked the gate and thrust his captive forward, keeping a grip on her arm.

"Good job, Mr. Miller," Sophie said. "I think the plan might just have worked."

The rocker lifted a trembling hand to push his long hair out of his eyes. "And good job to you, too, Sophie. I thought I was a goner there, until you knocked her knees out from under her. Are you okay?"

"Yes. She just stunned me a little." This was an exaggeration —a headache was gathering behind Sophie's eyes. "Let's go in and you can relax, take a shower. We'll let the team handle the perpetrators and the police. You can be last to give a statement."

"Sounds like a plan." Miller closed the gate behind the rest of them, sighing with relief to be inside the protected walls of the compound. "I need a drink. Please don't make me have one alone."

"We'll see." Sophie's knees were weak with reaction, too.

They staggered up the stairs, leaning on each other. Antigua met them at the open glass doors with a cry of distress.

"It's over," Miller said. "Thank God, it's really over." And the rocker collapsed into Antigua's supporting arms.

———

REVIVING MILLER, providing him with a drink, and sipping the hot toddy Antigua handed her, provided a respite for Sophie until Detective Cruz entered the den with Lei. "Sergeant Texeira wanted to come out when she heard the call on the radio."

The two women embraced briefly. "You okay?" Lei asked, warm brown eyes concerned as she looked Sophie over. "I heard the perp clocked you on the head."

"I'm fine. Nothing that an analgesic won't relieve." Sophie had her back teeth set against the pulse of a headache. "All went almost according to plan. We expected Blondie to be acting alone, however."

"About that, Mr. Miller," Detective Cruz said. "This is Sergeant Texeira. We'd like to take your statement."

Miller scooted to the edge of the chaise lounge where he'd been reclining, and reached out to shake Lei's hand. "Glad to meet any friend of Sophie's."

"Yes, I'm just here in a supportive capacity. Detective Cruz has been interviewing the suspects, but both are refusing to talk. We were wondering if you could come and take a look at them with the lights on—see if you recognize them. Only if you're comfortable with it, though."

"Hell yeah, I want to get a look at the woman who's been torturing me in effigy for months!" Miller made as if to bound up off the couch but Cruz held up a hand.

"Not so fast. Let's get a statement first." The stocky young detective took out a recorder and set it on the large glass coffee table. "Take us through the events as you experienced them."

Miller described the plan the team had come up with to flush Blondie out. "I didn't mind being 'bait' for this psycho. I was sick of the whole thing and if there was some way to flush her out of the woodwork, I was down with it." He described the action much as Sophie had experienced it. "Then, just when I was almost inside the compound, the bitch jumped out from behind a coconut tree and knocked Sophie off her feet." He looked down at his trembling hands, took another sip of a large tumbler of scotch over ice. "I tried to get the gate open, but I was too freaked out to remember the code, and while I was pushing buttons she hit Sophie with her gun, then grabbed me and pointed the gun at the back of my head. She's a big girl. I could feel she was as tall as me." He shuddered. "She whispered in my ear that we were finally going to be together, that nothing would keep us apart. Then Jake and the team arrived, and Jake told her to let me go. They had an exchange, which wasn't going well, when Sophie popped up off the sand and knocked Blondie's legs out from under her with a sideswipe kick." He lifted his drink in a toast to Sophie. "My heroine."

Sophie smiled. "We make a good team with Jake and our other operatives."

Miller nodded. "Anyway, Jake took her down after that, and here we are."

Cruz asked for a few more details, then stood up. "Well, we have a couple of officers ready to transport the two suspects, if you could just come and take a quick look?"

"Can't wait to," Miller said grimly, and stood up.

Sophie followed Cruz and Miller, Lei bringing up the rear, to the living room.

Seated on the couch, dressed in white tees and pants, hands behind their backs in handcuffs, were a man and a woman.

Sophie schooled her face not to react, but Miller reared back in surprise. "Amy? Bobby? What the hell is this?"

The woman, built narrow and dark-haired like Miller, dropped her head, shame in her posture. But the man, medium height with a bleached-blond mullet that reached past his shoulders, stared Miller right in the eye. "You just needed time with me to see that we were meant to be together, Simon."

Sophie belatedly remembered that Simon was Miller's given name as the rocker's mouth dropped open. Miller's throat worked, but no words came out.

Detective Cruz touched his arm. "So, you know these people?"

"Yes. Amy Miller. Bobby Miller. Cousins of mine from West Virginia." The color had drained from Miller's face. "I think I'm going to be sick." He spun on his heel and ran out, Antigua right behind him.

"We love you, Simon! Come back, let's give this a chance! The three of us are meant to be together!" Bobby Miller cried. "You just need to get in touch with your inner truth and you'll know I'm right!"

The door to Miller's suite slammed in answer.

Jake pushed off from the wall where he'd been leaning. "Let's give Mr. Miller the night off from the rest of this circus now that he's made a positive identification."

"We can do that," Cruz agreed. "Now which one of you wants to give your statement first?"

"I'd like an attorney," Bobby Miller said. Apparently, his delusion about Miller didn't extend to forgetting his legal rights. "And so would Amy."

Amy still didn't look up, but nodded in agreement. Sophie's mind whirled—*Blondie was a twosome!* So much for Dr. Kinoshita's psych profile. What had these twisted relatives planned to do to Miller? Hopefully some answers would be forthcoming, but not tonight, as Cruz gave up trying to get them to talk after a few minutes. "You two can spend the night in jail and we'll see you in the morning when your lawyers have been contacted."

Lei touched Sophie's arm as she followed Cruz and a couple of uniforms out of the house, escorting the prisoners to a police cruiser parked in the turnaround. "Before this case wraps up, you should come to dinner. Kiet would love to see his Aunty Sophie."

"Unfortunately, I'm going back to Oahu tomorrow." Sophie said as she hugged Lei goodbye. "And now, I need an aspirin and bed."

Chapter Thirteen

Sophie looked out the window of the Hawaiian Airlines plane at the ruffled cobalt surface of the ocean below, late in the afternoon of the next day. Maui rose behind her like a great green-gold turtle, clouds caught on its contoured shell. The short interisland flights were sometimes so low she could see whales swimming below—but not today.

Sophie had pulled together her few possessions and bade farewell to Shank Miller with many thanks and alohas. She had promised to return to train the AI software in a week or two, but in the meantime, she was anxious to get home to Connor and Ginger, and to give the FBI the limited intel she had on the Paradise Treasures connection to Assan.

She stared out the window for the short, twenty-minute flight, watching whitecaps sprinkled like faraway snowflakes on the ocean below, mentally reviewing the case.

She'd gone to bed with a pain pill, waking up logy and sore to a protein energy shake from Antigua and a "sitrep" meeting with their team. Bix piped in on Skype to hear the action resulting in Blondie's capture.

"We're asking Cruz to let me watch the interview with

Miller's cousins, but I don't think he'll allow it," Jake said. He was upbeat and energetic as usual, without even shadows under his eyes to hint at the stress of the night before—while Sophie felt tired, her head still tender. "We don't think much will happen with the interviews. The cousins would be smart to keep their mouths shut. I'm guessing their defense will focus on the fact that no actual harm was done to Shank or anyone else—even though Blondie was armed and tried to take him by force."

"Agreed. I think you should consider advising Miller to pursue a civil suit against these crackers," Bix said. "Wipe them out financially so they can't afford to keep threatening him."

"Crackers?" Sophie frowned. "I'm not familiar. A form of flat biscuit?"

"No. Hillbillies. Shitkickers. Rednecks. Inbred honky white trailer trash," Ronnie rattled off the slurs with the speed of memorization. *"Crackers."*

"Okay." Sophie jotted the words on her notepad. "I'm not sure what Miller's relatives' ethnicity has to do with their motivations regarding our client."

Bix sighed, loosening his neatly buttoned collar. Always a dapper man, this morning he looked a little tousled and irritable, even in the grainy feed of the Skype connection. "You're right, Ang. We shouldn't be generalizing. Still, someone needs to pull together profiles on these two, maybe even go out to West Virginia and do interviews with the rest of the relatives to help Miller build a case. I worry these two will be out on bail in no time. Even sentencing could just be a slap on the wrist."

"I can do the profiles for their online presences, but I'm not available to travel right now," Sophie said. Jesse put up a hand, volunteering to go, but Bix shook his head.

"Sophie, yes. Find out all you can about these two. But we need a seasoned interviewer to go to West Virginia and be our investigator. I'd like Jake to go, but I want to clear moving ahead with Detective Cruz first."

The meeting broke up after that. Sophie was off for another

week or so while the mansion's cameras collected data and Miller caught up with his rest. Sophie managed to dodge being alone with Jake when she bade the team goodbye until she came back to work on the AI.

Now, she sipped her complimentary passionfruit, orange, and guava drink, a fruity-sweet concoction known as POG, and let herself daydream about surprising Connor that evening. She'd pick up Ginger, go to her own place, get cleaned up, and then surprise him at the Pendragon Arches apartment. Maybe she'd wear that fancy underwear Marcella had convinced her to buy…

Her pulse sped up with anticipation.

Marcella and her fiancé, Marcus Kamuela, were happy together. Lei and Michael Stevens were happy. Maybe she and Connor could be happy, too, now that he was giving up his vigilante activities. She brushed Lei's observations about Jake aside —her friend didn't know the depth of what was between her and Connor. The Ghost was really the only thing that cast a shadow over her hopes.

She leaned her face against the plane's window, watching the ocean below beneath its scrim of whitecaps.

What, exactly, were her hopes? They were simple, when it came right down to it: waking up together, taking their dogs for a run, fixing breakfast, getting to work side by side at their computers, each with their headphones on…perhaps he'd ask her to move in with him.

Or they could find another place together, where their office wasn't a hidden room accessed through a closet. The thought made her smile.

Either way, being together, sharing space and a bed, sharing their lives, interests, and dogs—that was all she dreamed of or wanted. She didn't need to get married, and the idea of children terrified her. No, just to wake up in his arms in the mornings would be more than enough.

———

SOPHIE HAD LANDED and was waiting for an Uber at the Honolulu airport when her burner phone rang. Marcella's name showed up in the window.

"Sophie." Marcella's voice was tight and urgent. "Where are you?"

Sophie frowned at her friend's tone. "I just got in. I'm at the Hawaiian Air baggage, waiting for a lift back to my flat."

"Something's happened. I'll come get you." Marcella hung up.

Sophie canceled the ride and slid the phone into the side pocket of Mary Watson's floral dress. Her heart raced. *This could not be good.*

Marcella, sleek chocolate hair wrapped into a French twist, makeup immaculate, pulled up in her black Honda Accord fifteen minutes later. "I was headed downtown anyway so was able to get here quickly."

Sophie slid into the Honda's buttery leather upholstery and slammed the door, tossing her tightly packed duffel into the back. "What happened?"

"There's been an explosion at the Pendragon Arches building."

Sophie had envisioned terrifying scenarios involving Connor—but this wasn't one of them. Sophie buckled her seatbelt as Marcella pulled away from the curb, putting her cop light up on the dash. Sophie tried to calm her racing thoughts as they wove through the downtown Honolulu traffic. "What do you know?"

"Not much—but it's Remarkian's building, and his apartment floor."

"Oh no." Sophie shut her eyes, dizzy. The vibrant colors, sounds, and sights of a Honolulu afternoon spun by her. *Connor.* Her body was still imprinted with his touch. "No, I'm sure it's just a coincidence."

The black-edged terror churning in her gut took her straight back to the call she'd had about another man she'd almost loved —and had lost.

But at least Alika Wolcott was still alive.

"I don't know how much they will tell us at the scene, but I was working on the inquiry into his online activities that Lei told you about. I have a reason to go investigate." Marcella reached for Sophie's hand, a lifeline thrown to her as she drowned in churning emotion. "I'm so sorry, Sophie. I hate that he's mixed up in something that might have gotten him killed."

Sophie clasped her friend's hand, squeezing it hard. "I don't know what I will do if it's Connor." Her lips felt stiff. Hot and cold sensations flashed over her body. She pressed her forehead against the cool glass of the window.

"I know." Marcella squeezed her hand back. "Let's just take this one minute at a time."

Chapter Fourteen

The fire investigator and the head of the Honolulu bomb squad met them in the lobby of the Pendragon Arches. The detectives assigned to the case, unfamiliar to Sophie, greeted Marcella like a long-lost colleague even though she was FBI. Marcella's fiancé was an HPD detective. Her friend probably knew all of the downtown staff by now.

"We need to know what apartment was involved in the explosion," Marcella said. "We have a witness in one of these apartments."

Smart of Marcella not to expose Connor to the other investigators. A remote part of Sophie's brain appreciated her friend's agility and tact from an investigative standpoint.

"The explosion occurred late last night, and the blast was localized to one apartment." The fire investigator gave the number.

Connor's apartment! Sophie's stomach clenched. She pushed a fist into her abdomen, swallowing bile.

"We're still checking for structural damage." The fire inspector clapped his hard hat back on after running a hand through sweat-damp locks. Sophie kept her face carefully neutral, breathing shallowly, as the man went on. "Our crews have already had a look inside. One male victim."

"That was our witness's apartment," Marcella said tightly. "Sophie knew the occupant, Todd Remarkian. Do you have an ID on the body?"

"No. Subject is still unidentified." All eyes fastened on Sophie as she pushed away from the wall.

She could feel the tightness of her skin, the wide, dry expanse of her eyes. "Yes, I knew Remarkian well. I can identify him."

The bomb squad chief shook his head. "No one can go in or out until we're sure the ceiling won't collapse. We are waiting on Dr. Fukushima, the medical examiner, to come and assess the body on site. We'll give you a call as soon as we know more. Wait for word from us."

———

SOPHIE DIDN'T REMEMBER Marcella driving her to her little incognito Mary Watson apartment. She didn't remember Marcella tucking her in bed, handing her a sleeping pill and a glass of water, and closing the door. She didn't remember anything until she woke suddenly to a leaden sensation of dread.

Something terrible had happened. She groped to remember it, but like chasing mist, it evaded her.

Sunlight smote her eyes. *Marcella had not closed the blackout drapes.* Sophie turned her head and looked out at an offensive, blinding blue sky that mocked her with a beautiful Honolulu day.

Connor was dead.

The realization burst across her brain, reverberating.

Sophie covered her head with a pillow and rolled into a ball, letting the pain out in a howl that clenched her guts. The howl turned to sobbing. She sounded like a trapped, wounded animal, and she pressed the pillow harder to her face to muffle the ugliness, smothering herself. Colored dots filled the black of oblivion as she pressed the pillow tighter…

"I've brought someone who is very happy to see you." Marcella's voice impinged on the darkness.

Ginger, ninety pounds of freshly washed, energetic yellow Labrador retriever, leapt up onto the bed, nudging aside the pillow and licking Sophie's tear-stained face. Sophie reached up with both arms to embrace the dog. Ginger's tail lashed her, the dog's ecstatic whimpering cries calling her back into her body, into the present. Marcella's voice came from the doorway. "I'll leave you two to get reacquainted. And I'll be in here, fixing some heavy carbs for breakfast."

Sophie patted the bed beside her, and Ginger lay down. Sophie wrapped her arms around the Lab's sturdy neck, breathing in her warm doggy smell as she cried. Gradually the harsh sobs abated and her body relaxed.

The smell of pancakes and bacon, along with Ginger's coaxing to play, finally drew Sophie out of bed. She wrapped herself in her favorite dragon-embroidered robe and shook her head as she sat down at the little dining room table in front of a plate mounded with pancakes. "Whatever have I done to deserve you as a friend?"

Marcella kissed the top of Sophie's head, embracing her with one arm, spatula still in hand. "I'm Italian. When we're stressed, we cook. I have some lasagna noodles started for later."

Sophie's belly was knotted, but she couldn't refuse her friend's kindness. She dug into the mountain of pancakes and Marcella joined her, biting into a crisp piece of bacon.

"Any news?"

"Nothing yet."

The answer was enough to allow Sophie to finish eating. Marcella handed her a mug of strong tea as she cleared the empty plate. "I lied. I wanted you to eat breakfast. Dr.

Fukushima wants us to come down to the morgue and identify the body."

Sophie breathed carefully to keep her breakfast down and wrapped nerveless fingers around the mug. "Let me take a shower and get ready. I can do it. I have to see him. I have to know."

Chapter Fifteen

D r. Fukushima, the medical examiner, met them at the door of the morgue, opening the automatic door by hitting the button with an elbow. The ME was much as Sophie remembered from her FBI days: a small, tidy woman, self-contained, with kindly eyes above her surgical mask. Today she was engulfed by a blood-stained, wraparound rubber apron and topped by a chef's hat.

Marcella gestured to the white paper hat. "What happened there?"

"I ordered proper head coverings, and this is what I got. The hospital wouldn't let me return them because we couldn't get a credit." Fukushima shrugged. "It's here to hold the hair back, and it works. Come see our victim." She cut her eyes to Sophie. "Agent Ang. How are you the next of kin?"

"Just Sophie, please. I've left the Bureau. I don't know that I am his next of kin. But Todd Remarkian had a very small circle of friends, no family that he ever disclosed to me…and we were dating." Her throat closed. *So much more than dating…*

Dr. Fukushima fiddled with her apron tie, a nervous mannerism Sophie had never seen before. "I'm sorry to have to ask you to do this, then. Perhaps we should just go by the dental records."

Marcella's voice sharpened. "You have dental records?"

"They're on the way. We wanted to rule out the occupant of the apartment, first, and it was easy to contact Todd Remarkian's dentist—Security Solutions had the names of his medical providers on file."

"I need to see him." The words burst out of Sophie, pressured and harsh. *Whatever the damage to his body, she'd recognize him.* She had to see what remained for herself.

"I just wanted to spare you, if that was possible. But I see that it is not." Fukushima made a gesture with her head, and the two women followed her through the open morgue area. The distinctive morgue smell, a potent blend of chemicals and decomp, clung stickily to Sophie's throat.

Sophie smelled the burnt flesh and hair of the draped body before they reached it. Marcella ducked her head, holding up an arm to breathe into her elbow. "Phew."

"The victim was fairly close to the blast. You won't get much from his face, so perhaps it's just the body you want to look at." Fukushima glanced up at Sophie. "If you think you can recognize his body."

"We had sex a number of times, so I think I can recognize it." Sophie's voice sounded flat and mechanical, even to her own ears. *What a statement to describe such sublime lovemaking.* Her eyes felt dry and she made herself blink.

Fukushima lifted the blue paper covering partway.

"Remove the whole thing, please."

Fukushima pulled the covering off entirely. Marcella gasped and turned away.

The body on the table was burned over every inch. A good deal of the midsection was gone, including the groin area. An arm was missing. And the face was…*simply not there.*

A pulp of charred flesh covered white gleams of bone where

his face should have been. A few teeth remained, unlikely pearls in a meat stew.

Sophie stepped up to the corpse, breathing shallowly through her mouth so as not to inhale the ripe odors rising from the body.

This was the only chance she would have to discover if this was really Connor.

She found it surprisingly easy to detach. She bent close, assessing.

The overall shape and size of the body were right.

The height was right, judging by the measurement markings on the side of the table.

Sophie moved in close to peer at the head.

A tuft of short, ash-blonde hair, the right color to belong to Connor, clung to the sphere of bone that remained of his skull.

Sophie moved around to the remaining arm and pointed to the hand. "Were you able to get any fingerprints?"

Fukushima grasped the arm and turned it outward so that Sophie could see that the digits were burned down to the bone. "I retrieved the missing arm, but it's in even worse shape than this one."

Sophie stood back, getting an overall proportional impression. She thought back to their recent, memorable night together. *Connor walking toward her, naked, and rather magnificent.*

No tattoos, little body hair, and no birthmarks. Wide shoulders, chiseled muscles, well-turned legs—his perfect proportions were, in themselves, distinctive.

The mutilation of the corpse before her made the body difficult to compare to that vibrant memory.

Sophie scanned down the legs to the feet.

They had spent time in bed, teasing each other, getting to know each other's bodies, tickling each other's feet. She shut down her mind on that tender, playful memory. *If there were anything left of his toes on the right side, she'd know for sure.*

The toes were gone on that side, sheared off as if with a

sharp instrument.

Sophie swallowed bile for the first time. "What happened here?"

Fukushima bent, dropping magnifying lenses over her goggles. She grasped the stubs of remaining toes, and spread them, peering close. "There was a lot of very sharp debris in the apartment. I can have the crew there look for a piece of metal or glass that could have done this." She crooked a bloody finger for Sophie to come closer, and Sophie leaned over to look at the one remaining toe.

Bone gleamed in the raw flesh.

"His foot was covered by something when we arrived at the scene. I have to check my scene photos to be sure, but I think it was the steel sink from the kitchen. It apparently sheared the toes off. And it could also explain why this area is not burned." She pointed at the pulpy end of the stub of toe, blistered but not burned.

Marcella had gone to lean against the wall. "Do you recognize him, Sophie?" Her voice sounded tight and small.

Sophie never took her eyes off the body. She gestured toward the door. "I'll meet you outside when we're done, Marcella." She barely registered the sound of the door closing.

"I can do some further tests, check this area for explosive residue. He was wearing a white martial arts robe that had plenty of residue on it." Fukushima indicated a bloody, soot-darkened pile of white material on one of the tables. The sight made Sophie's gut clench—that robe had been Connor's favorite garment to wear in his apartment. "Took me forever to get the fabric remnants off the body."

"What kind of device was it?"

Fukushima frowned. "I would tell you more if I could, but all I can say is that it was a small, well-placed and deadly bomb."

"I understand. I forget I'm just a witness in this investigation." Sophie straightened up. "So, what you're telling me is that you're not able to discern if this injury to the foot was pre- or post-mortem."

"That's what I'm telling you."

"What about DNA to help identify the remains?"

"Of course, I have taken samples." Fukushima shook her head. "But they're only as good as a matching sample from the victim procured for comparison."

"So, I take it there's nothing in the FBI or HPD identification base that matches Todd Remarkian?"

"No." Fukushima tidied the area around the body reflexively, wiping a stain, stowing implements. "I already requested, and there was nothing on file."

Sophie couldn't think of any biological residue Connor had left behind that would yield enough of a sample. She'd checked out of the hostel, where she might have recovered a stray hair with a root bulb. Connor had never spent the night at her Mary Watson apartment; in fact, she had hidden that address from him. But he *had* stayed over at her father's apartment for an extended period when she was recovering from a gunshot. *Perhaps she could find something there, if the maid wasn't too thorough.* Still, it seemed unlikely.

"I can have the fire investigators check thoroughly for any useful DNA in the apartment," Dr. Fukushima said. "And the investigators can look in his office. But I'm pretty sure there's not going to be a sample on record with any law enforcement agencies."

Connor would have made sure of that. He would not want any record of his DNA on file with any agency of any kind, nothing that could tie him to the many suspicious deaths he was associated with. Nothing would be found in his apartment, either, most likely.

Sophie jerked with the suddenness of a thought. *What about the "Batcave," his second, hidden apartment next door? And... what had happened to Anubis?*

"Did they find a dog's remains in the apartment?" The

thought of intelligent, elegant Anubis, burned and forgotten in the debris, knotted Sophie's stomach as much as looking at the corpse before her.

"No. No dog." Fukushima glanced at her curiously. "Why?"

"He had a dog." Sophie felt tears pressing against the back of her eyes for the first time as she looked down at the body on the table. "A beautiful dog."

"Maybe it's at a dog sitter, if it wasn't at the apartment."

"I will look into that." Sophie lifted her eyes to meet Fukushima's. "In the meantime, can you let me know what the dental records confirm, when you get them?"

Fukushima shook out the drape and snapped it over the body with a practiced gesture. "Of course."

Sophie left her burner number with Fukushima, and joined Marcella out in the hall. The FBI agent was on her phone, pacing the dimly lit hall outside the morgue entrance.

"Thought you were going to have the doc redo the post, with you present." Marcella slid her phone into her pocket, and gave Sophie a steady look. "You don't think that body is him, do you?"

Sophie did not respond. Marcella was investigating Connor for the FBI, and Sophie was investigating Connor's death in her own way. The two were not compatible.

She needed to get rid of Marcella so she could find Anubis, and hope her friend hadn't already thought of the missing dog. When she found the Doberman, she would know more than that charred body would ever tell her.

"I need some time alone. I hope you understand." Sophie let some of the emotion she'd locked down show through her eyes as she met her friend's gaze.

"Of course." Marcella enfolded Sophie in a hug.

Sophie suppressed a twinge of guilt and closed her eyes to savor the firm support and loyal friendship she felt in that embrace, and then detached herself gently. "I'd appreciate a ride back to my place."

Chapter Sixteen

S ophie found Anubis at the first place she looked: the same kennel she used for Ginger. The woman in the facility's records office, whose brass plaque identified her as Bernice, frowned as Sophie showed her Security Solutions ID. "Mr. Remarkian never told me he wasn't coming back for the dog."

"Of course he didn't. Nobody expects to get killed until it happens to them." Steel in Sophie's voice caused the woman to quickly consult her files.

"Every dog owner has to fill out an information sheet and designate a next of kin to pick up the dog in case the owner cannot return," Bernice said, clicking away on her keyboard.

"I am aware. I keep my dog Ginger here, as well."

"Of course!" Bernice's manner warmed, became sympathetic. "We love Ginger."

"That's right. Marcella Scott is my next of kin for Ginger. I don't know who is for Anubis, but that person should be informed of Mr. Remarkian's death."

Bernice tapped the line in question on her screen and looked up at Sophie over her half-glasses. "You're Anubis's next of kin, Sophie Ang."

SOPHIE TOOK both dogs for a run through the city from Mary Watson's apartment down to the long swath of Ala Moana Park spanning the beach at Waikiki. She didn't let herself think about what it meant that she was Anubis's guardian until the dogs were loose in the fenced dog park, delighted to be reunited, cavorting and enjoying the sunshine. Anubis's elegant carriage and dignified mien was a foil for Ginger's uninhibited, cheerful charm, and Sophie smiled in spite of everything at the playful wrestling of the two. They seemed as happy as long-separated siblings to be reunited.

Connor had planned this.

He had chosen her to be his partner, his woman. *His dog's guardian.*

She wouldn't be surprised if the whole thing wasn't smoke and mirrors. He could be watching her right now through some hacked surveillance cam, sipping a margarita on a tropical beach in Belize.

No. Connor wouldn't be sipping in careless comfort. He'd be tortured by regret, but he'd be watching, nonetheless. She and his dog weren't his priorities. *The Ghost was.*

The FBI was getting too close, and he'd cut his losses and run.

Or, he was dead.

She was not sure which felt worse to contemplate.

Sophie sat down on the bench, looking out at the peaceful, turquoise sea, gilded with afternoon sun and ruffled by a gentle breeze. The cooing of doves and chattering of mynahs in a nearby monkeypod tree should have been soothing, but only wound the knot in her belly even tighter.

Either he had faked his death, in an elaborate scheme with multiple stages of planning, or Connor really *was* dead, at the hands of some unknown enemy.

What did it say about her relationship with Connor that,

now that she'd picked up Anubis, she was more convinced he was faking his death than that he'd really died?

Either way, the only feeling she could muster about the body in the morgue was a numb sense of betrayal. Her response to the corpse she'd examined had been nothing but detached coldness, a clinical analysis that had raised even Dr. Fukushima's brows.

Sophie tipped her head back and closed her eyes, trusting the dogs to warn her of any hostiles, and concentrated on what Connor would have had to do to fake his death.

He'd have had to find a body that was a virtual double of his own, keeping it frozen until the time was right. He'd have had to set up the dental records with teeth matching that of the cadaver. He'd have had to cut the toes off the corpse, eliminating the only truly individual thing about his own body, and create a plausible reason for the toes to be gone. He'd have had to deal with his money, his affairs, and his dog. He'd have had to clean out any and all DNA from his apartment and workplace and other venues, and he'd have had to build a bomb big enough to decimate his apartment, but small enough not to cause any other damage to the building.

He'd have had to thaw the body, staging it out and placing it where it would get maximum damage in an explosion. And then, he would have had to disappear after he set off the explosive, wiping all evidence of his activities and identity.

All this to avoid detection by the FBI, so he could keep being a vigilante. The part of Sophie that still hoped Connor was alive shriveled within her.

If he was still alive, he'd fled just when she could have used his help and support, facing the threat of Assan.

And if he was capable of all of those things, of setting her up to grieve, of having to go through identifying his body, then he wasn't someone worthy of her love.

And then there was the alternative: *Connor really was dead.*

And while the Ghost had plenty of enemies, the one most likely to have blown him up was Sophie's ex.

She hunched over suddenly, curling around a white-hot ball of agony that tightened her gut. Was it even a physical pain? She couldn't tell.

"Are you all right?"

Sophie opened her eyes, still hunched over her folded arms. A woman approached her, but stopped as Anubis stepped in front of Sophie, growling, his lip raised over a row of gleaming teeth. Sophie snapped her fingers and pointed to the ground beside her, as she'd seen Connor do. The Doberman sat beside her, docile, as Ginger galloped up to the woman, wagging her tail.

"I'm fine. Thanks for asking, just a bit of bad fish last night." The dog owner smiled back, patting Ginger's head, and went off after her own dog.

Ginger turned to lick Anubis's face, a gesture so like a kiss that Sophie's heart constricted. How could Connor leave her like this, just when they were getting started as a couple?

She was cursed to live alone and die alone. She was poison to anyone who tried to love her…

The black maw of depression yawned before her, a depthless hole drawing her in. Soon she'd dive into it, and be lost.

She had one more thing to do before she gave in to its pull.

———

Sophie walked into the computer lab of the University of Hawaii with her laptop under her arm. Wearing Mary Watson's floral exercise wear and a pink hoodie, she plugged in the laptop, hooked up to the data stream, and booted up DAVID.

Sophie kept big, light brown Jackie O sunglasses on as she cycled through her surveillance caches, looking for anything new on Todd "Connor" Remarkian, as well as the Ghost.

No activity on any of his credit cards, personal accounts.

She had expected that—but not discovering that when she pulled up his ID, his middle name was listed as Colin, not Connor.

Was even the private name he'd given her a lie?

Sophie hacked into facial recognition at the airport, running an FBI program she'd kept a copy of. While that ran, she searched for his name on all incoming and outgoing flights in the last week.

Nothing, of course. *He'd have an alias.* Maybe a dozen of them. And he was excellent at disguises.

She tried combinations of his name, knowing he was too smart for that, but driven to try, anyway.

She planted a spyware program on the airport surveillance feed and set it to ping to her phone if the recognition program identified him.

But what about ocean travel?

He wouldn't go that way. Too slow, too vulnerable on a boat, too trapped if something "went sideways" as Jake called it.

Sophie imagined Connor sitting in the "Batcave," as they'd called his secret lab, activating his departure measures that included destroying his rigs and accessing a bug-out bag of new identity, funds, and disguise. They had never discussed it, but she knew he had one.

Because she had one. She was already using it. But she had another one set up after Mary Watson, and she wasn't half as paranoid as Connor was.

She set some new keywords on DAVID, checked for anything new on Assan. Nothing there, either.

Time to take a break, and go check for clues in the "Batcave."

Chapter Seventeen

S ophie walked down Connor's familiar hallway. It reeked of smoke and the chemical aftermath of fire suppression.

She'd taken extra care in disguising herself for the surveillance cameras embedded along the hall outside the door of Connor's apartment. A large sun hat and a velour jogging suit over a towel wrapped around her middle distorted her body shape, and an auburn wig hung past her shoulders. Bright pink athletic shoes that fastened with Velcro tabs were consistent with the look.

She walked quickly past Connor's door, crisscrossed with crime scene tape, to the adjacent apartment that he rented under a different name.

Even though this one wasn't sealed, she had to work fast in case the watchman downstairs was actually paying attention. Wearing thin latex gloves, her back to the camera, the large brim of the hat hiding her activity, Sophie jimmied the door with her lock picks and slipped inside.

Pitch black with the power out, the apartment reeked of smoke.

Sophie switched on a small, powerful flashlight and walked

through the open, empty living area to the bedroom in back, a room connected to Connor's apartment by a door concealed in the closet between the two rooms.

She flipped the light switch, but of course nothing happened.

If he were going to leave her a message, it would be here.

She walked up to the computer bay where Connor spent the most time. Three monitors in his work area gleamed in the flashlight's beam, three more in hers. The desk that wrapped around one side of the room was characteristically tidy. She shone the light around, but the area appeared undisturbed. *She'd have to take his computers to know anything more.*

There wasn't time to clone his hard drives, nor power to support that process, so she'd take them manually. Dropping to her knees, Sophie took a small toolkit out of the backpack she'd carried in and unscrewed the panel of Connor's main rig. A few minutes later she'd disconnected the hard drives running that computer and stowed them in her bag. He'd set up a computer area for her to work on as well, and she took those hard drives, too.

The foul air stung her lungs. *She had to get out of there; every minute that went by was one more that she could be trapped in a compromising position.* She paused for one last look around the space, for anything out of place, any clue he might have left.

A landscape postcard, of a towering, contoured green valley ending at a cobalt sea, was stuck on the wall over the main monitor in her area. *"See Kalalau, Kaua'i!"* the caption across the front trumpeted.

Connor would never just thumbtack a postcard onto the wall. He was precise and careful about his personal space—he'd tuck a memento like this somewhere, or use two-sided tape that wouldn't ruin the paint to hold it. *This could be a message.* Feeling her belly flip, Sophie reached out and pulled the thumbtack, taking the postcard down, turning it over.

Nothing on the back.

Her breath whooshed out and her knees buckled at the disappointment.

Of course, there was no message. He had to assume the investigators would find this place—but apparently, they had not.

She stuck the postcard in the bag and left the way she'd come, hurrying to the stairs and all the way down multiple floors out of the building, not taking a deep breath until she was outside and well down the sidewalk.

Chapter Eighteen

After taking the dogs for a quick walk, Sophie hooked up the hard drives and activated them—but nothing would come up but a staticky white screen.

They'd been wiped, probably magnetically. *Was it possible that was related to the explosion?* Nothing could be retrieved—more evidence that Connor could be alive. He'd never want his computers to fall into anyone's hands! But maybe he'd had a backup measure that wiped them automatically if there was a threat to his system? There was just no way to know.

Sophie pushed away from her desk in the bedroom, swinging back and forth in the chair, studying the postcard in her hand.

Maybe he had left her a message, maybe he had not. Nothing she had found so far was definitive either way—and did she want to keep looking for a man who was either dead, or had let her think he was?

The soul-sucking loss, grief, and depression gnawed at Sophie. And now, she had nothing to hold it back.

No one knew where she was, and that was just how it should be.

She closed the laptop, unplugged it, and barricaded herself

and the dogs inside Mary Watson's apartment, activating her security measures. To avoid worries that Ang had captured her, she recorded a message on the burner's outgoing voice mail that she was sick. She shut the blackout curtains, and went to bed.

Three days went by.

Sophie slept, cocooned and smothered in darkness, only responding to the dogs' needs for food and exercise by staggering out twice a day for short walks.

An insistent pounding on Sophie's door, accompanied by the buzzing of her phone surveillance app, woke Sophie on the fourth day. She picked up the phone and saw Marcella's face in the video cam window. Marcella was the only person who knew where Mary Watson lived. *Damn it!*

She got up, undid the locks and chains, and lurched back to bed. Light striking her eyes woke Sophie further as Marcella yanked the blackout curtains wide.

"Sick, my left tit." Marcella put hands on her curvy hips. "I knew you'd be in bed. Wallowing."

"Why did I ever show you Mary Watson's apartment?" Sophie rubbed her face and pushed her hands into her cropped hair. It felt greasy and matted.

"I know you're grieving, but Jake was driving us all nuts down at the office. I told him I would verify that you were still alive." Marcella sat down on the bed beside her. "That guard dog of Todd's didn't even bark when I was pounding on the door. He knew you needed rousting."

"Anubis is very intelligent, and he knows you." Sophie looked over at the dogs. Anubis and Ginger sat by the door, ears pricked, clearly hopeful she was going to take them out.

She tried to remember when she had last taken them out.

Yesterday evening. Yes, definitely yesterday. *And she had fed them too.* She wasn't so far gone that she would let the dogs suffer. "Well, now that you've seen that I'm alive, would you mind closing the curtains?"

"Of course, I mind! You don't get to check out of life just

because your boyfriend did." Marcella winced. "I'm sorry. That came out harsher than I meant it to."

All that Sophie couldn't say about Connor and his "death" choked her. *But if she told Marcella about the Ghost now, it would either continue the manhunt against him, or the Bureau would be chasing a literal ghost.* No, she had to keep sitting on the secret, and it was one more reason to be angry with him.

Sophie swung her legs off the side of the bed and stood up. Her head spun, and she sat back down again.

"When did you eat last?" Marcella was already heading for the kitchen. "Never mind, don't answer that. Go get in the shower. You stink."

Marcella sounded just like her mother. Disobeying peppery Anna Scatalina was out of the question, too.

Under the fall of water, Sophie felt herself slowly regathering from the dark place she had gone, re-entering her body as if fitting back into a too-tight glove. Her fingers traced along the delicate tracery of her tattoos. *Hope. Respect. Power. Truth. Freedom. Courage.* She could live with those, even if she never got the *joy, love,* and *bliss* circling her navel.

She had to go back to the things that had worked in the past to beat her depression…or it might drag her under, and never let her go.

Her mother, a lifelong depression sufferer, was now permanently placed in a treatment facility in Thailand, semi-catatonic. Thoughts of Pim Wat's severe symptoms prodded Sophie to keep moving. She shaved her legs, oiled her skin, conditioned her hair, dried off, wrapped herself in her robe, and joined Marcella in the dining nook.

"You look better." Marcella handed Sophie a mug of tea. "Breakfast is on the table."

An hour later, with a plate of scrambled eggs and chopped veggies topped with cheese tucked into her belly, Sophie felt almost human again. She drank the strong tea, and each sip seemed to bring fresh vitality into the husk of her body.

"Thanks, Marcella." Words she wanted to say, about how her friend went above and beyond the normal balance of friendship, caught in her throat like burrs. "I don't deserve you."

"Of course, you don't." Marcella burped behind her hand, setting her fork down beside her cleaned plate. "But I love an excuse to invade your place and feed you. Mama taught me well. Now, when are you coming back to work?" Marcella pointed at the phone, plugged into the charger. "Jake says he needs you over on Maui."

A tiny fern of interest uncurled inside of Sophie. *What could be wrong with the case?* She thought it was wrapped up. "I'll call him." She swallowed a fortifying swig of tea. "Any positive identification on the body at Pendragon Arches?"

"Yes. The dental records confirm the body as Todd Remarkian." Marcella put her hand over Sophie's. "I'm so sorry."

Sophie felt nothing. *She'd expected that.* "What about DNA?"

"Weirdly, we can't find any viable DNA from Remarkian at the apartment. Even with the explosion, it's pretty odd. I was hoping you had something that the crime lab couldn't find." Marcella looked pointedly around the apartment. "But I don't see anything of his in this apartment."

"I have no doubt you already looked through the cupboards and my bedroom." Sophie quirked a brow at her friend. "I never brought him here."

"Not ready for that level of commitment?" Marcella's cocked head and big dark eyes reminded Sophie of an inquisitive blackbird.

Sophie stood up and cleared their plates. "We were just starting a relationship. I was a long way from telling him about Mary Watson."

But Connor had known about Mary Watson, anyway. He probably knew where her apartment was, too. Her shoe size, her bra size…there wasn't a thing about her that Connor hadn't known or couldn't find out if he wanted to—while he had managed to make sure he left nothing—not even DNA —behind.

Nothing but his dog.

Her heart lurched at the thought. Connor had loved Anubis, and he'd left the dog to her. *What did it mean?*

"Well, we need a warrant to send a lab team into your father's apartment where he did spend some time with you, unless you want to just let us in there?" Marcella asked.

Sophie nodded as she washed up the dishes. "You can have the key. I'll call my father and let him know the FBI will be going in looking for trace."

"I'm guessing a few of the messages on your phone are from your dad, too." Marcella sipped her mug of coffee. "He must be worried sick."

Sophie shrugged. *She was doing the best she could, and that had to be enough.* Frank Smithson, after living with her mother all those years, understood. He'd told her that as long as Sophie let him know she was okay, he could live with her periods of silence and withdrawal. But if longer than a week went by, and he had reason for concern, he would send whoever he could find looking for her.

She had reached that limit.

"I owe him a phone call, anyway." Sophie turned, and opened her arms to her friend. "I'm ready to get on with things. Thanks for understanding that I needed a little time out."

"You're entitled." Marcella's hug was fierce, and smelled of the pikake perfume she had taken to wearing. "You can always count on me."

———

SOPHIE CALLED her father as she drove to the gym late that afternoon. "I'm sorry it's taken so long to get in touch with you, Dad."

"You were reaching your check-in limit, my girl." As usual,

her father's warm, deep voice filled her with a sense of reassurance. *The world couldn't be that far off-kilter with Francis Smithson in it.* "I was getting ready to activate the emergency network."

Sophie chuckled, an unfamiliar sound. She cleared her throat. "Well, I was on Maui with a case and then…the man I was dating was killed." Saying the words, telling someone who mattered to her about Connor's death, made the situation she'd been struggling with bloom into stark reality. Tears filled Sophie's eyes, and her hands trembled on the steering wheel as she braced herself to explain the circumstances to her father.

His exclamations and rapid-fire questions hit her like bullets, but she forged ahead, describing how a bomb had gone off in Remarkian's apartment, and that she now had not one, but two dogs. "The FBI needs to get into your place to look for any trace related to identifying Remarkian's body. It's improbable that anything remains from his stay there, but I hope you'll allow that."

"Of course. I'm so sorry, darling." Her father sighed, long and low. "You've had an unfair amount of grief to bear in this life."

"I believe that to be true. I'm unlucky."

"No, Sophie, no." His protestations made no difference to the truth she knew in her bones—even as the rational part of her mind argued it was another myth, part of the depression.

Sophie pulled into a parking stall outside of the strip mall housing the gym. The bright sunshine of another day in paradise smote her sore eyes as she removed her sunglasses. "I'm all right, Dad. I'm going to the gym. And then I'm returning to Maui for my case. It will be good to be working again."

"I've always found work to be a tonic," her father agreed. "I'll be over for a visit in a couple of weeks. We can spend some time together then. Are you staying in the apartment?" Frank had encouraged her to live in his penthouse apartment in the swanky area of Nu'uanu, and Sophie had lived there for the first five years she was on Oahu and in the FBI—but recent events had turned a former sanctuary into a place where she felt vulnerable.

"No, Dad. I'm at my other place. We'll talk soon." She hung up before he could argue with her about that, too. He didn't like her identity as Mary Watson, nor the run-down area where she'd rented her off-the-grid apartment.

Sophie looked around the brightly lit, modern interior of her new gym. Mary Watson could not go to her old, beloved gym, Fight Club, with its dim, barnlike lighting and many memories. This new place, Fighting Fit, would have to do.

Hitting the heavy bag sent reverberations through Sophie's whole body, each blow like striking a drum.

Amazing how quickly she'd gotten out of fighting shape.

She changed up her combination: right hook, left jab, right uppercut, left cross. And again, and again.

She was shaking and sweaty way too soon.

Might as well lie down and wait for Assan to come get me. No point to any of this. The intrusive thought sucked energy from her body, weakening her muscles.

No.

She'd go down fighting. She'd survived this long; she'd survive again.

Sophie lowered trembling arms, took off the gloves, and picked up a weighted jump rope.

She managed to keep going for fifteen minutes.

The manager, a short Filipino man with a hard, compact rubber ball body, came by to check on her. "You seem to know your way around the bag. Do you spar?"

"I would definitely like to spar with a partner. I do MMA and boxing. But I'm going to be out of town for a while."

"Okay. Let me get your name and some contact info. I'll let you know if I come up with any female partners for you."

"They don't have to be female. I've fought men before, and done just fine."

"I believe that." The manager raked Sophie with a glance.

She felt out of shape, but her body still looked good: five foot nine inches, a hundred thirty pounds of muscle and bone, honed by recent weight loss.

She'd regain the strength she'd lost as soon as she put the time in.

"I'm Bernie Costa." The manager extended a meaty hand.

"And I'm Mary Watson." Sophie gave him the burner number and Mary's email. "I'll be back soon. I like it here."

And she did. Because she'd remembered something important, beating on that heavy bag.

Chapter Nineteen

The Bank of Hawaii branch Sophie headed for was located downtown, shaded by monkeypod trees among swanky shops and busy sidewalks. Sophie parked Mary's humble white Ford truck at the curb shaded by one of the huge, iconic trees. She left the dogs in the cab, their heads hanging out of rolled-down windows.

Walking into the bank, Sophie flipped through Mary Watson's ring to the shiny brass key she'd noticed but hadn't put there. *When had Connor left the key there for her to find?*

She remembered the day he'd made a point of asking her to stop outside this bank so he could run in and make a deposit. She hadn't paid attention at the time, but he never did anything that wasn't purposeful. When they'd begun dating, he'd told her he was going to add her onto his safe deposit box "in case anything happened to him." *Well, it had, and sooner than either of them was ready for.*

Inside the bank, Sophie rubbed her hands on the skirt of Mary's coral-colored halter dress, a garment she'd donned after showering at the gym. A normal boyfriend would have brought her here and had her sign a form… *Damn Connor.* Why couldn't he have been like everyone else?

But she wouldn't have fallen so hard for him if he were.

Sophie went up to a customer service representative in the New Accounts area. "Hello. I need to get into my safe deposit box."

"Sure." The woman rose, smoothing down a muumuu printed with bananas and leis. "Follow me. What's the number?"

"That's the thing. I'm sorry, I can't locate it. My name is Mary Watson. Here's my ID. And my key." She handed both over, her face as neutral as she could make it.

Putting the key on Mary Watson's key ring was his way of sending her another message…about what name he'd listed on the box.

"All right. Just a minute while I look that up." The woman walked behind the counter and Sophie heard the rattling of the keyboard, then she pushed a book toward Sophie. "He filed an extra paper with a copy of your ID so you didn't have to come in and do a signature card."

Sophie's heart squeezed. *So much secrecy. So much planning.* Was this thoughtfulness, or was it deceit, betrayal?

She signed the line next to the time in the book with Mary Watson's signature, and the woman handed back her ID. "Follow me."

Sophie's heart beat with heavy thuds. Would he have left her a message in the box?

The vault was chilly, and echoed with the sounds of their footsteps. The rep found the numbered box, inserted her key, put in Sophie's key, and turned them both at the same time.

"You can take your box out and put it back yourself," the woman said. "And booths are available in the corner for privacy." She pointed to three curtained alcoves against one wall.

"Thank you." Sophie waited until the woman walked out, then removed the lidded drawer, and went into the curtained booth.

She lifted the lid and removed a sealed envelope, bulky with an object inside, *SOPHIE* written on the envelope in Connor's tidy script.

She tore the envelope open with trembling hands. The rectangular block of a small external hard drive fell into her hand from inside a curl of paper. She slid the hard drive into her purse and unfolded the note.

"Dear Sophie:

If you're reading this, I've had to leave you, by death or necessity... and you must be furious with me. I imagine being in your shoes, wondering what the hell to do next. All I can tell you is that I'm sorry. If I went...or if I died (which amount to the same thing), it wasn't my choice. I wanted a lifetime with you.

Please don't waste time grieving, or looking for me. You won't find me. I'm dead or gone... Please move on, as quickly as possible. I want a future full of love for you—you deserve it, after all you've been through, and it hurts me to have added to your pain.

My estate is left to animal charities; I will not burden you with dealing with that. The Ghost software is my real legacy, for you to do with what you will. I hope you can find a way to use it for the kind of good you can live with, and if you destroy it, I understand that, too.

After all, it's the reason I'm no longer with you. I would never leave you if I had a choice.

I love you and always will. There was only ever you, for me.
~Connor"

Sophie crumpled the note, her eyes flooding with tears. "Damn you, Connor. *Damn you to the plagues of the tenth ring of hell!"*

She wanted to throw the Ghost hard drive on the ground and stomp on it with all the rage and pain coursing through her. Instead she cursed, in Mandarin, and Spanish, and Thai, and she tore the note into tiny, tiny bits—and just when she was going to sweep them into the handy trash can, blinded by tears, she knew she'd want to read his words again.

She swept up the fragments and dropped them into an inside pocket in her purse. She wiped her eyes, replaced the drawer, and left the bank.

Connor was dead.

And even if he was alive, he wasn't coming back.

Chapter Twenty

Back at her apartment, Sophie inserted the external hard drive she had retrieved from the safe deposit box into her laptop. She flexed fingers, leaning in to examine the files as the drive opened.

But it didn't open. An access code window popped up, instead.

"Son of a two-headed yak," Sophie swore. Of course, it was coded. But he'd left it for her. What would he know that she knew, that no one else would?

The thought was so intriguing that it reminded her of one of the online flirtations they'd indulged in before they met in person.

And now he was dead.

There would be no more games, no more flirting. No more intoxicating moments in his arms. No more working companionably side-by-side in the "Batcave."

There was only Sophie looking for answers, and a future that felt bleak and doomed to end at the hands of a man who'd sworn to kill her.

The pain was overwhelming.

She pushed the pain and the memories away, into that dark place where she kept Assan—and now that lockbox contained Connor, too. She focused on the little blinking cursor in front of her instead.

Sophie ran through a series of dates first: the first time they went out together. The weekend they spent in Hana. Their first date at the Bishop Museum. Her birthdate, something she had never told him but was pretty sure he knew, like he knew everything else about her. She tried dates with initials, dates with names, dates with their dogs' names. Frustrated, she pulled up one of her password-breaking programs and set it to work.

She refused to dwell on the dull throb of betrayal she felt looking at the blank, empty place where an access code belonged. She needed to think like Connor. *What would he have done?*

But she'd never had much of a window into his clever and devious mind, and even trying to imagine thinking like Connor hurt too much right now.

She turned off the codebreaker program, closed the laptop, and put it in her backpack. Bix had left her a message that he was sorry for her personal loss, but she was needed on Maui at the Miller estate.

Work would have to suffice as a reason to go on living.

Chapter Twenty-One

Sophie hadn't been able to return for the Miller job in Wailea until she'd closed her affairs and boarded the dogs, all of which took a couple of days. Leaving the animals at the kennel had been difficult—but there was no place for them at the Maui job, where she intended to immerse in work. She was already as attached to Anubis as to Ginger. Something about the way the dogs needed her, the way they accepted her no matter how she was feeling or acting, brought solace and kept her moving forward.

Sitting on the Hawaiian Airlines flight to Maui had begun to feel routine, but this time, sipping the plastic container of passionfruit-orange-guava juice handed her by the flight attendant was disorienting. *She'd been so happy on her last flight, looking forward to a break from work and seeing Connor.*

Today her body was a mass of aches after a sparring session with a Tongan woman the previous evening at Fighting Fit. The bruises and throbs were familiar, a return to a known state of body and mind after a brief hiatus to somewhere happier.

The aircraft bounced in strong trade winds funneling between the two volcanoes that formed the Valley Isle, and swooped in over a quilt of colorful sugarcane fields, a distinctive sight. The sugarcane industry was coming to an end, but the fields still waved gracefully in the wind for a while longer.

Jake met Sophie at Maui's open baggage claim, driving the Tacoma loaded with ocean equipment that Miller kept for his vacations on the island. Her partner unlocked the vehicle's door without getting out of the cab. Sophie tossed her backpack into the truck bed and got in.

Jake was in his usual all-black combat gear, and she felt leashed tension vibrating off of him as she settled herself. "Get in a fight I don't know about?" His steel-gray eyes assessed her. "Your ex make another run at you I didn't hear about?"

"No. Just getting back into my old sport. Enrolled in a new gym. Got a sparring partner yesterday that gave me a workout." Sophie touched the swollen corner of her mouth where the Tongan had landed a good punch. "Like old times."

"I see." Jake looked away and pressed down on the accelerator, pulling out into the busy traffic that flowed around the airport's open design. She'd ignored all his attempts to reach her since she left, and she felt his hurt like an accusation, vibrating in the air between them.

"I'm sorry I was out of touch."

"And I'm sorry about Todd." Jake's hands clenched on the steering wheel.

"What for?" Sophie kept her eyes on the changing scenery. "Todd is the one who died."

"'I'm sorry' is what you say when a friend suffers an untimely loss." Jake glanced at Sophie. "But you seem to be taking it well."

"I cared more about him than you know, but it's not something I want to talk about with you. Or anyone." Sophie twisted her hands in her lap. The fragile bubble of detachment she was cultivating threatened to burst, leaving her showing emotion in front of a man she was determined to keep a distance from.

Long moments went by as Jake navigated the Kahului traffic

and got on the long straightaway of the Mokulele Highway toward Shank Miller's estate in Wailea. Finally, Jake said, "I was worried. Tell me more about what happened."

"It's an ongoing investigation, but everything points to Remarkian being dead of a small, targeted explosion." Sophie kept her voice expressionless. "The fire inspector says it was a small IED." Sophie stared out the window, the sugarcane fields rolling by, a backdrop to her thoughts. There was nothing she could say about Connor that didn't lead into more unanswered questions.

"Who do they think did it?"

"They have no idea. But I think it might have been Assan. He had the last man I dated almost killed, and I'd only kissed him."

"It's not your fault. You aren't responsible." Jake squeezed her arm with a big warm hand, and she wished she could let him comfort her—but nothing good for either of them lay down that road.

"Tell me what's going on with the Blondie case. I'm here to work."

"Fair enough." Jake said. "Well, in addition to training the AI, the case against Miller's cousins is getting complicated. Bobby Miller's out on bail already, and both of the cousins refuse to talk or make any statements. Don't forget, they lawyered up early. Dr. Kinoshita thinks they might go after Miller again when they are both out."

Sophie's heart rate picked up. "Unbelievable that their attempt could be that blatant and the authorities don't take it seriously."

"It's not that they don't take it seriously. Lei and Cruz are as frustrated as we are. It's that this kind of case seems to favor the stalker. Kinoshita is advising Miller to go after the two of them in civil court and wipe out their financial resources, but he won't do it."

"Survivor guilt?" Sophie glanced at Jake. "Miller feels bad

that he's wealthy and successful and so many members of his family aren't?"

"It could be partly that. But I suspect it's something more…personal."

"Like what?"

"Like he might have had a relationship with those two in his foolish youth."

Sophie sat up and turned to face her partner. "Did he tell you that?"

"No. But I know him pretty well, and I can tell he's hiding something about them and feels guilty. Too guilty to go after them the way he needs to."

Sophie touched the side of her head. "Amy hit me hard. With a gun. I'll testify to that."

"Of course. The assault is indisputable, as are the threats we all witnessed. But they are not enough to put Amy away for long. And Bobby? They've got nothing on him but criminal harassment."

Sophie frowned. "So, Miller's safety continues to be a concern."

Jake nodded, turning the truck onto Piilani Highway, the long straight stretch leading to Kihei and Wailea. "Hence my asking for you to come help—in spite of your bereavement. And I thought it might be a distraction for you."

"Yes. Work is good." Sophie sighed. "To make matters worse, if possible, the FBI still hasn't found anything on Assan."

Sophie'd held back telling Marcella about her lead on Assan and visit to the Paradise Treasures Gallery because she wanted another look at it, now that the gallery had left a message that her art piece was framed and ready for pickup. "I have a lead on Assan that I haven't shared with law enforcement. I wonder if you'd be willing to go follow it up with me, give me a second opinion."

Jake's eyes were fierce as they flashed from the road to meet hers. "Anything I can do."

"I need that support, thanks. I started pursuing this lead, but am not sure there's much there. It's thin. But it could be a connection to Assan here on Maui." She described her visit to Paradise Treasures. "There was nothing conclusive, but this seems like the kind of thing Assan would do—loan this gallery owner cash so he's able to hide his money there, and have her provide a cover for him in return. I didn't find anything concrete, just had a feeling something was off. The owner was… alert, I would say, to any probing. Now I have to go back to pick up my art piece. Going as a couple would throw off anyone looking for me."

"You got it. When do we go?"

Sophie smiled. "How about tomorrow? If you can get the time off from Miller."

"It's a date."

"No, it's not, Jake. We are *not* dating." Sophie burst out harshly.

He slanted her a look. "Of course. Just a figure of speech."

"I must be clear. I'm not dating anyone. Ever again." Sophie's fists clenched in her lap. "I'm done with men."

"I'm sorry you've had such a rough time," Jake said quietly. "It's not fair and it sucks. I understand why you feel that way."

Sophie looked out the window at the pretty plantings and open vistas of Wailea, pressing her bruised cheek against the window. The pain felt good.

———

"I'M SO SORRY. Your boyfriend. It's awful." Antigua gave Sophie a warm hug in the entryway of Miller's mansion.

"Yes." Sophie still struggled to find the proper thing to say in a situation like this. "Am I still in the guest room?" Jake strode purposefully down the hall, carrying her bag in that direction. "I guess so."

"You can have any room in the house that would make you

feel better." Shank Miller descended wide, bleached-wood stairs from his master suite atop the house. "Including mine."

"That is kind, but it would not make me feel better." Sophie could tell by Miller's downcast expression that she should have said something different. "But it is nice of you to offer. I am fine in my usual quarters."

He reached her. "I felt terrible when I heard what happened."

"Yes," Sophie said again. Her response felt inadequate, like she'd been handed a script and a part to play for which she had no proper lines. "You are being compassionate, but I am here to work."

"Of course you are. But not tonight." Antigua still had a hold on Sophie's hand, and squeezed it. "Tonight, Shank and some of his band are going to entertain us. Right, Shank?"

The rocker pushed his long locks back. "We're just doing a jam session. Practicing. But we wanted to give all of you the evening off to hang out. Drinks and food will be featured, right, Antigua?"

"Of course."

"You don't have to do that." Sophie's words still felt stiff, her body wooden. "I am not in need of entertainment."

"I wouldn't think of trying to entertain you. I'm the boss, remember? But I have to keep up my skills, and I require an audience." Miller had a dimple when he pinched his mouth shut on a smile.

Jake reappeared. "And you are forbidden to work this afternoon because I've started a system upgrade on the computers, too. Out to the beach with you, to soak up some rays. It's a gorgeous day." He gestured to the glass doors, open to the broad stretch of beach framed by palm trees. Sophie had been anticipating her escape into the cyber world, but she had to admit the beach looked tempting as she walked to the doors.

"I'll come with you," Antigua said.

"Me too," Jesse chimed in from the door. Already clad in

surf trunks, a towel over his shoulder, the young security agent grinned. "Security Solutions looks after its own." Sophie couldn't miss the bulge of a weapon in the small black bag that Jesse carried. She was carrying protection, too.

Surrounded by the support of co-workers that had become friends, Sophie felt herself finally begin to relax. *Taking an afternoon and evening off was maybe not such a bad thing.*

———

SOPHIE WAS warm and relaxed from an afternoon at the beach, sitting on the lawn in one of the sun chairs with Antigua's interpretation of a Blue Hawaiian in her hand. Shank and his bandmates tuned up their equipment on the wraparound deck of the mansion, and Sophie leaned her head back, closing her eyes.

"Sophie!" Her friend Lei's voice roused Sophie from drowsing.

She shot up off of the low chair to embrace her friend. "Lei! How great to see you. And the family, too!"

Lei had brought her tall, broad-shouldered husband, Michael Stevens, who carried their baby Kiet in his arms, and even Lei's father, Wayne Texeira, brought up the rear of the little cavalcade, hefting a diaper bag.

"Well, we could hardly ignore an invitation from Shank Miller to come to a home jam session," Lei said, as the rocker grinned and lifted a hand in greeting from the porch, striking a dramatic chord on his guitar.

Stevens embraced Sophie. "So sorry to hear all you've been through."

"I was just sick when I heard about Todd!" Lei exclaimed.

Sophie's eyes filled and her throat closed, but baby Kiet, on Stevens's hip, reached out his little arms for Sophie and provided a great distraction. "Oh my, young man, you are getting so big." Sophie tightly hugged the beautiful child with his green eyes and black hair. "Come sit here with Aunty Sophie."

Soon the informal concert was underway, drawing a crowd of beachgoers to cluster around the outside of the clear Plexiglas surround, clapping and cheering. Inside the compound, a warm and festive feeling pervaded the intimate group. Sophie watched, listened, and snuggled Kiet. Jake and Antigua, Lei and Stevens, Wayne and the friends Miller had invited danced on the grass below the deck, while Shank Miller showed them all why he was a superstar.

Chapter Twenty-Two

S ophie looked at the bright, shiny yellow Bentley convertible Jake sat in, parked in the turnaround the next morning. She raised her eyebrows. "Don't you think this is a little flashy?"

Jake pushed a button and the convertible top retracted, settling with a smooth slithery sound into a holding cradle behind the bucket seats. He stroked the leather-bound steering wheel appreciatively.

"Now it's flashy. Perfect for a rich couple in love to take out for a spin to an art gallery in Lahaina." Jake hoisted himself out of the low-slung car, trotted around to the passenger side, and opened the door for Sophie. Wearing a white linen shirt and worn, expensive jeans with a pair of broken-in loafers, Jake looked every inch of the successful businessman going some-where casual. "Shank made me take this car. Said he wants to buff out his favorite pair of security agents. Hop in."

"This is the first time in months I've seen you in anything but work clothing." Sophie felt a smile tag her lips. The grief over Connor continued to sap her energy and strength, and even her beach afternoon and the wonderful jam session last night had failed to banish the sorrow weighing her down—this was the first minor lift she'd felt since the news. "Well, if Miller authorized it."

She slid down into the sleek sports car's buttery leather seat, tweaking Mary Watson's sundress down over her knees. Jake closed the door with a gentle click. "This dotcom magnate is off to pick up some high-end art with his beautiful girlfriend." He got in on the driver's side, starting the Bentley with a push button.

Sophie flipped down the visor mirror to dab red lipstick on her mouth. "I don't know about beautiful, but we look the part otherwise." The scar on her face was still hard to see past, pulling her eyes out of alignment, marring her cheek.

"Of course you're beautiful." Jake's voice was rough. "Never doubt it."

"You don't have to get that much in character," Sophie said stiffly, flipping the mirror back up. "No one to see us here but Antigua, and she wouldn't like you flirting with me."

"A sincere compliment. Not flirting." Jake hit the remote for the gate. He whipped the car out onto the road, driving so fast Sophie had to hold her straw hat on her head.

Sophie's spirits lifted as they spun through the curving streets of Wailea, sheltered by tall monkeypod trees, and she laughed aloud as Jake really opened the sports car up along the stretch of highway fronting Sugar Beach in Ma'alaea.

"Driving a Bentley, we can afford a speeding ticket," Jake shouted over the rush of the wind, his grin back in place.

Sophie smiled, holding her hat, as the car hugged the curves around the cliffs of the Pali.

The ocean was a sparkling cobalt mystery far below, the cliffs above already golden and dry, dotted with black lava rocks. A row of towering white windmills cresting the ridge reminded Sophie of a giant's playful pinwheel. All of the landscape's contrasts showcased Maui's unique features. *She was glad to be here.*

Way too soon, they pulled up and parked in the tiny lot

behind Paradise Treasures Gallery. Sophie ducked her head, allowing Jake to close his door, swagger around the front of the attention-getting car, and open hers. Jake took her hand and lifted her out of the seat. He kept hold of her hand as he closed the door behind her, and leaned over to whisper in her ear.

"Relax. We're just playing a part."

"Of course." Sophie loosened the tight grip she had on her straw bag and allowed Jake to lead her inside and encircle her waist with an arm as they walked into the cool depths of the gallery, heading toward the back area where she planned to pick up her art piece. They browsed slowly, pausing to take in the various sculptures and art on the walls, both of them scanning for any revealing details.

A woman dressed in one of the gallery's Grecian gowns approached them. "What can I help you with today?"

"We are just looking around. I am here to pick up a piece I was having framed," Sophie said.

"And I would like to see if we need anything new for the house," Jake said. "We're going to be done with the place before you know it, honey."

Sophie smiled up at Jake. "And you said you would leave the decorating to me. *Honey.*" She turned back to the saleswoman. "The owner, Magda Kennedy, helped me last time. Is she available?"

"I'm sorry. She isn't on the floor today. What was your name?"

"Mary Watson."

"I'll go fetch your painting." The woman rustled off.

Sophie moved away from Jake, but he trailed his fingertips down her arm to take her hand again. As she turned to look at a piece on the wall, his warm, solid presence at her side seemed to thaw some of the ice around her heart. *She had a friend who was there for her no matter what.*

Her mind ticked over his actions and words since she'd arrived—he was being thoughtful and kind, his flirtiness gone.

She could trust him. He was involved with Antigua now, and that was a good thing.

The saleswoman brought the painting out. Sophie unwrapped it to check the framing and show it to Jake. He exclaimed enthusiastically over the composition and subject matter, and Sophie was surprised by the acuity of his observations. They rewrapped the painting. "Tell Ms. Kennedy I will be back," Sophie said.

The saleswoman smiled. "She will be so pleased."

Settled in the car, still parked between other vehicles, Sophie turned to Jake. "Well, what did you think?"

"I think that gallery has a lot more going on than meets the eye. Art is a great way to launder money, and that place had some big names, really upscale pieces. More than that, it's very secure. I spotted a service elevator behind the counter. I bet the place has multiple floors that are used by the business." Jake started the Bentley and began to pull out.

"I agree." Sophie tilted her head, frowning at a low, persistent hum increasing in volume. As they cleared a large van, backing up to head out of the lot, Sophie's eyes widened at the sight of a large, helicopter-style drone heading their way. The spider-like device appeared heavy-duty, with six whirling propellers on extended arms zooming it rapidly toward them from behind the building. Weaving slightly, it settled to the rear of them, a targeting light blinking from the metal protrusion at its apex.

"Get us out of here, Jake!" Sophie cried. "That drone is armed!"

Jake hit the accelerator and the Bentley bolted forward so quickly that Sophie's hat flew off, blowing away across the back of the car as he burned rubber. Sophie fumbled in her bag, her fingers curling around the cool pebbled grip of her Glock.

The *ting!* of a silenced bullet hitting the back of the Bentley made her scoot down in her seat instinctively, rolling over in the foot well to sight up the back of the seat as Jake whipped a left turn out of the parking lot onto a side street. The drone followed, another *ting!* hitting the expensive car just behind the convertible cover.

Sophie took aim at the pursuing mechanism and fired. *Bam! Bam! Bam!* The sound of her weapon was deafening down inside the shell of the car's body.

The drone stuttered and wove back and forth—she had hit one of the rotors—but it stabilized and fired again.

This time the windshield cracked. Jake jerked the wheel in reaction and cursed. Fortunately, no traffic interfered as Jake floored it, heading for an intersection. "Going right, hang on!"

Sophie fired again. *Bam! Bam!* just as Jake peeled the vehicle to the right, throwing her against his leg. The drone heeled to one side and zigzagged off, its flight uneven.

"I think I hit it! Let's go back and try to retrieve it!" Sophie yelled.

Jake hit another right turn, careening around the block, but a tourist bus blocked their way and oncoming traffic prevented any further speeding. It was several moments before they were able to return to the place where Sophie thought she'd hit the drone. Parking the convertible, they both got out, weapons drawn, and walked down the block, searching and alert. The quiet residential street with its overarching mango trees and smell of dusty sunshine contrasted jarringly with their deadly situation.

"Here!" Jake called Sophie from the opposite side of the street from her. Sophie hurried across the road to meet him, glad of the low-heeled, strappy sandals she'd worn with Mary Watson's halter dress.

Buried deep in the broken branches of an oleander bush, the drone hummed and vibrated like a fly captured in honey. The weapon function clicked, out of ammo. Jake reached in under the device and pushed a button, and the remaining propellers stilled at last.

Jake extricated the twenty-inch round metal contraption. "I

think we can assume your ex sent this after us. Unless there's someone else out there who's trying to kill us with expensive and hard-to-obtain equipment."

"I believe you are right." Sophie took the damaged weapon in her hands and hefted it. Slender arms, each topped with a propeller, branched out from the drone's central body from which the weapon section protruded. "Looks like police or military grade. Not customized."

"These can be bought on the black market." Jake's eyes were steely with anger. "This perp nearly got us. And he sure as hell got Shank's Bentley. We need to inform the cops at this point."

Sophie nodded reluctantly. "Yes. But can you keep my lead on Paradise Treasures quiet a little longer?"

"No. This happened directly after our visit there. No way that's a coincidence. You need help getting this guy, Sophie."

She thrust the drone into Jake's arms. "Or I'll have to just get him myself."

"How, exactly? He could have been anywhere in the area operating this thing, or had someone else do it. This kind of drone uses a virtual reality headset paired with hand controls operated on a touchpad. What we need is the cops to get here and canvass the area for anyone who might have had that kind of equipment."

"Like he's still here." Sophie paced back and forth, amped up, her eyes scanning the nearby buildings. "Or ever was. I can't see Assan leaving his comforts, even to try to gun me down."

A plan was forming in her mind.

She would cooperate with the police. And then she would find another way to get to Assan, now that she was sure that Paradise Treasures held the key to his location.

Chapter Twenty-Three

Lei frowned at the shot-up Bentley and the mangled drone flyer as Detective Cruz wrestled the unwieldy metal contraption into a large evidence bag. They'd dusted it for prints, but had found none but Sophie's and Jake's. "This is a new way to take a shot at someone. Pretty high-end."

Jake nodded. "These are not easy to come by, even on the black market."

"First time I've even seen one of these on Maui," Lei agreed.

Officers were already out canvassing, looking for any witnesses who might have seen someone flying the drone, and Sophie and Jake had given their statements. Sophie had also updated Marcella and the Oahu team on the phone.

She leaned against the side of the shot-up Bentley, impatient to get a shower and move on with her plan. "It's my ex, Assan Ang. No other explanation makes sense."

"Likely. Though we don't know if it was Ang or someone working for him. He could be thousands of miles away right now," Jake said.

"He's not. He's here." Sophie paced in a shallow pool of

shade in the parking lot of Paradise Treasures. She had reluctantly shared the tip she had on the gallery, and heard from Lei
that MPD had had dealings with the gallery owner, Magda
Kennedy, before—but the woman had always come out clean.
"Can you bring in the gallery owner?"

"Kennedy's got a heavy-hitting lawyer. We can't pull her in
for something so thin. Plus, she's not a talker. We've grilled her
hard before and never got anything useful," Lei said.

"I know she 'came out clean' as you said, but is she the
kind of woman who might get involved with Assan
for money?"

"Quite possible. Her gallery was used for mob money laun-
dering, which she pinned on her manager—but I was never
convinced she didn't have something to do with it or some
knowledge of what was going on. We just couldn't make it stick
to her."

Sophie gestured to the car. "Can we get this poor vehicle to
the police impound and go back to Miller's? I need a shower."
Her body was sticky with post-adrenaline sweat.

"Yes. We'll let you know if we get anything," Cruz said. Jake
thanked him and got into the vehicle, but Lei put a hand on
Sophie's arm.

"Why don't you ride with me? I'll take you back to Miller's
and we can talk in my truck."

Sophie nodded and walked over to Jake to tell him the plan,
while Lei did the same with Cruz. Soon the two women were
walking toward Lei's silver Tacoma. Sophie got in, removing a
plastic rattle and setting it in the child's car seat in back of the
extended cab. Surrounded by more toys and a diaper bag, the
area attested to baby Kiet's frequent presence. "It was so great
to spend time with Kiet yesterday. How'd he do with such a late
evening?"

"Just fine. He pulled himself up to stand in his crib this
morning." Lei settled herself in her seat, putting on her belt and
turning on the vehicle, adjusting the air conditioning. "He keeps

us all on our toes. Thank God Stevens and I have my dad to watch him while we work."

"I envy you your family." Sophie looked out the window, embarrassed by the words that had spilled right out of her heart.

Lei touched her shoulder. "I'm so sorry. You've had an unfair share of heartbreak."

"People keep saying that." Sophie said. "It is not helpful."

Lei pulled out of the parking lot and got on the road. "I'm not supposed to tell you anything, but Marcella and I agreed that it might help with your grief to know that we have reason to believe Todd was using his position and access to tech at Security Solutions to be a sort of…online vigilante."

Sophie tried to look surprised as her heart thudded. "What?"

Lei narrowed her eyes. "Yes. I understand from Ken Yamada that you were the one to connect Sheldon Hamilton with the vigilante calling himself 'the Ghost.' Later, Ken suspected that Hamilton wasn't the real perpetrator."

"Really."

"You knew." Lei eyed Sophie shrewdly. "I can see that you knew."

"I…suspected." Sophie looked away, sighed. "What does it matter now? He's dead." Sophie gazed at her friend, letting her pain show, letting her eyes fill. "I even thought I loved him."

"Oh, Soph." Lei reached for Sophie's hand. Sophie leaned her head on Lei's shoulder as she drove. She breathed in her friend's scent of coconut oil and baby powder, and finally straightened up.

"I knew I was taking a big risk getting involved with him." *It felt good to tell her friend what had really been going on.* "But there was no way to prosecute him, as I'm sure the FBI will find. That I even discovered the Ghost was purely a result of my use of DAVID, an unauthorized program. He was too careful. Too good at what he did. And he believed in what he did. Sometimes I did, too."

Lei pulled the car out onto the main road. They drove for a few moments in silence.

Finally, Lei said, "I can see why he was so attractive to you. He was the total package: brilliant, rich, good-looking. He was no ordinary criminal."

Sophie hated to hear that word used to describe Connor, but technically, it fit—as did the rest of Lei's description. And yet, none of those words captured Connor's complexity, his passion, his heart.

"Did he have anything to do with that FBI agent's death?" Sophie asked.

"That's still inconclusive. But there are a number of open FBI cases that I think the Bureau would like to lay at the Ghost's door." Lei sighed. "This is difficult, Sophie. Just because he's dead doesn't mean there aren't still questions that need to be answered."

"I would appreciate it if you could find some way to get me off the witness list, if this talk today could be off the record. Please. I think I've already been through enough with this, don't you think?" Sophie knew she was putting Lei in a bind, but it was one she'd been living with, herself, for months. "He's dead and gone. What does it matter, really? And the really sad thing is…" She swallowed, went on. "The sad thing is that he finally said he'd give up the vigilante activities because I asked him to. He wanted a future with me."

"Damn it." Lei touched Sophie's arm. "I will do my best to keep your confidence. But I can't promise someone won't want to drag you in for more questioning to close a case." She wove between a truck loaded with pineapples and another weighed down with surfboards. "Do you have any ideas who might have killed him?"

"Assan is the first person who comes to mind," Sophie said. "After what happened to Alika, I believe Assan plans to target not just me, but any man I show interest in. Hence today's attack on Jake and me. We were posing as a couple in the gallery, and I think it enraged him enough to try to take out both of us."

"Someone needs to nail that bastard," Lei said.

"On that we agree."

They arrived at the estate, and Lei let Sophie out in the turnaround. "I better get back and help Cruz. I don't have much hope we'll catch Ang on the streets of Lahaina, but we have to do our due diligence."

"Maybe you'll get lucky. Someone has to know something about where he is," Sophie said. "Thank you for…keeping my secret."

"I'll try, that's all I can promise," Lei said. "Now go soak in a hot tub or something. This mansion must have one." She waved as she drove off.

———

ASSAN PACKED the VR headset and controls back into their molded plastic case. His hands were shaking with the aftermath of rage and frustration.

He should never have tried to use his toy on his wife and her newest lover, but the sight of them in the gallery had been too much. Self-control was important, except in those situations when he could really let his inner demons out.

The weaponized drone was a sample that his black market arms dealer friend had given him to check out for importing. He hadn't been able to resist sending it after them.

Jealousy had clouded his thinking. The drone had almost shot Sophie, which would have spoiled his fun—and now he'd tipped his hand that he was in the area for sure. Soon the place would be crawling with cops. His window to capture Sophie was closing.

But he bet that she'd ditch her supports and come looking for him—and he'd be ready.

As for the cops—he loved the United States! Their laws that protected criminals were so helpful. They would have to have probable cause to search this building, and there was no way they would get that.

Still, he had to destroy the case and the controls.

He picked up his phone and hit a number in his Favorites.

"What do you need, Mr. Ang?" Magda Kennedy's voice was cool, smooth as poured cream. *He'd love to get that haughty bitch tied spread-eagled on his sex wheel, screaming—but not with pleasure.*

"I need to dispose of something confidential. It must be destroyed in the next hour. And I would like a woman." *His anger had to go somewhere.* "Someone who likes things rough and can keep her mouth shut."

A long pause.

"That will cost you extra," Kennedy finally said.

"I expect no less."

She ended the call.

Assan paced in front of the sliding glass windows of the penthouse, annoyed by the sparkle of the sun on the ocean across the street, the sounds of vacationers that wafted up from below. *Maui was so shallow.* Nothing about its garish beauty and vacation charms had any substance. He couldn't wait to get back to Hong Kong, a place of depth, mass, and complexity, a truly stimulating environment where anything and everything was available and possible.

A buzz at the door brought him to check the peephole. He opened the door to one of Kennedy's minions, a blond man in the gallery's uniform of white shirt and pants. "You have something to be disposed of, sir?"

"Yes. Dispose of this where it can't be found." Assan handed the man the sealed cardboard box he'd put the controls into. "Keep the box shut and make sure no one ever finds the site."

"You got it." Blond Boy took the box, and then extended his hand.

The fool wanted a tip.

Assan took out his wallet and slapped a hundred-dollar bill into the man's hand. "Doesn't she pay you?"

"Not enough for projects like this." The young man's hand remained outstretched. Assan put two more hundred into it and the man closed his hand. "This is going straight into a trash compactor."

"Good."

Blond Boy left as Assan's phone buzzed. He picked up.

"I have a number for you for that other thing you wanted," Kennedy said. "But you didn't get it from me." She rattled off the number. "When will you be wrapping up your time on Maui?" Disgust for him colored her chilly voice.

"When my business here is done." Assan hit the off button. *Kennedy was going down.* She'd be the last thing he took care of when his business with his wife was complete. She was disrespectful—and she was a loose end.

He called the number she'd given him, and soon entertainment was on its way.

Chapter Twenty-Four

The mansion did have a hot tub. After another couple of seemingly endless hours meeting with Shank Miller about the attack, helping Jake call the rocker's insurance company to put in a claim on the Bentley, and updating their team and Bix on Oahu, Sophie was exhausted. She slid into the warm water of the bubbling tub tucked under a gazebo of jade vines in a corner of the estate. She closed her eyes, leaning her head back to rest on the rim.

She felt wrung out, twisted, empty. The depression urged her to just slip beneath the water.

Sophie battled the negative thoughts with difficulty. *She had to stay focused,* finish her job with the AI here at Miller's, and wait for the dust of the investigation in Lahaina to settle so she could implement her crude plan of attack against Assan.

"This seat taken?" Jake's voice.

She didn't open her eyes. "As you can see, the area is vacant."

"Just another figure of speech." She heard the sound of the water shifting as he slid in, the sigh of contentment he gave.

She didn't want to like that tiny, vulnerable sound. Didn't

want to wonder if he looked as good as she knew he did in just a pair of swim trunks. She didn't want to admit that she felt better with him there, the shadows pushed back by his presence. But she did know all these things, and resented them.

She was done with men. Period.

"What did Lei want to talk with you about?"

"Just a recap on the case." She wasn't telling Jake anything about the Ghost.

"Did she have a plan on what to do next about your ex?"

"No." Sophie opened her eyes to stare at her partner. Unfortunately, Jake did look as amazing in a pair of swim trunks as she'd anticipated, with his ripped arms spread along the rim of the tub, his gunmetal eyes at half-mast as he watched her. "I came here to relax. These questions are not relaxing."

"Sorry." He sighed again.

Sophie shut her eyes, and he said no more—but she could feel him watching her, hear every tiny shift of the water lapping against them. She couldn't take it anymore. "Why don't you go see Antigua? I'm sure *she'd* like to spend time with you."

A long pause.

"If that's the way you want it." Jake's tone was chilly. She heard the rush of the water as he got out, the pause as he picked up his towel, the wet padding of his feet on the paving stones as he walked away.

Sophie gave in and slid under the water until heat and the need to breathe forced her back up to the surface. She got out and rinsed, then went back to her room. She plugged into her computers and worked steadily on the AI training and integration until she was nodding with tiredness.

Someone knocking loudly finally got through the thunder of classical music in her headphones and she went to the door. A tray sat outside containing a small clay pot of curry, half a papaya with lime, an array of fresh steamed vegetables, and a flask of strong tea.

Antigua was a kind and thoughtful woman. *A good foil for Jake.* Hopefully, he realized that.

Sophie picked up the tray and withdrew back into the room.

She slept, eventually, and got to work again in the morning, looping in video from all over the house, running probability ratios and behavior norms. At last, she booted up her own laptop and DAVID and cycled through her search caches, looking for any sign of Assan or of Connor.

Nothing. The frustration almost made her scream.

Around noon of the next day, Sophie was done with her work on the AI. She stretched her arms above her head, picking up her phone.

The burner showed multiple calls, but Sophie hadn't set up a voice mail, so she scrolled through them and returned Marcella's call first. "Marcella. You rang me?"

"Yes. Just wanted to check in about the attack that happened yesterday? Lei said you think it was Assan. She told me you had intel pointing to a gallery in Lahaina. Why didn't you tell me you had a lead?" Marcella's voice rose on the end of her question.

"I wanted to handle it myself." Sophie got out of her chair, stretching stiff muscles, and dropped to the floor to do some yoga poses while they talked. "It was a very thin lead. I did an initial recon before Todd was killed and got nothing, so I didn't tell you about it. I took Jake for a second look—and I think we triggered Assan. Literally."

"So, you and Jake were—what? Canoodling?"

"Canoodling?" Sophie frowned.

"Kissing. Getting handsy. You know. PDA—public displays of affection."

"Hardly. He held my hand, though, and put his arm around my waist. We were impersonating a couple. I was worried I'd alerted the owner to my interest in the gallery on my other visit, and wanted to throw her off." Sophie pushed a hand through her short, dense hair.

"So, you're telling me that you think your ex has some kind of surveillance set up at the gallery, and that the mere sight of you and Jake holding hands was enough to have Ang send out a weaponized drone to blow you away?"

"That is what I think. Yes. And that is also why I think Connor was killed by Assan."

"Connor?"

"Todd's middle name. Or, I should say—the name he told me to call him. Because his legal middle name is Colin, which I found out after his death."

"So, how much did you know about his online activities?"

"I can't talk about that."

A short, sharp silence.

"There is a lot about this guy you haven't told me, Sophie." Marcella's voice was tight with hurt and the quick temper Sophie had only encountered a few times.

"There is a lot I will never tell you, or anyone," Sophie said evenly. "The FBI will have to conduct their investigation into Todd Remarkian and his online activities without my help. I hope that won't be a problem with our friendship."

"It is right now." Marcella ended the call with an angry click.

Sophie stared down at the little burner phone in her hand. "You can count on me," she said, repeating Marcella's words. But she felt her friend's frustration and betrayal, too.

Another reason to hate the Ghost.

Sophie got up and packed her belongings, checking the clock. She'd been enclosed in the room for close to twenty-four hours, and had finished the AI training. She sat back down and typed out a quick list of instructions for monitoring and responding to the software, disabled the camera overseeing the den, and opened her door carefully.

No one in the hall.

Sophie carried her tray into the kitchen and set the note on the island in the center, anchoring it with a chunk of rock crystal.

There was no way she was sneaking out of the compound unseen, but she'd chosen the hour the security staff met for their daily briefing, and they'd be too occupied to come out and question where she was going or what she was doing. She took a large cloth beach bag out of the hall closet along with a beach towel, and went into the den.

Weapons issued by Security Solutions were stored in a metal transport locker with a combination lock. Sophie consulted her confidential app containing the agency's passwords, and a few moments later had the lock open.

Sophie took out several weapons and their holsters along with a couple of boxes of ammo, and wrapped them in the towel. She added some surveillance equipment, slipping everything into the canvas bag. In Mary Watson's sundress, the bag slung over her shoulder, she looked like she was headed for the beach.

But where she was going, no one could follow.

Sophie had just slung her backpack of personal belongings and the beach bag with its heavy burden into the trunk of the ugly Dodge rental when Shank Miller, wearing workout clothing, his hair tied back in a ponytail, approached her. "Where you off to?"

"Mr. Miller. I'm sorry, I have some urgent personal business."

"I'm sure." The rocker leaned on her car door, preventing her from closing it. "We're concerned about you. Shouldn't Jake be going with you?"

"No, he's right where he's supposed to be—running your security." Sophie forced a smile. "I'll be back shortly. Just a little errand. I'm done with the AI and left instructions for the team in the kitchen." She gave the door a tug. "Goodbye, Mr. Miller, I will see you soon."

"Stay safe," the rocker said, frowning. She nodded and

started up the car, pulling out and away before he could try to prevent her exit.

She had a lot to do to get set up, and not many hours of daylight left.

As the compound's gate retracted, Sophie began to pull forward—but hit the brakes when a large black motorcycle, engine revving, bore down on her, weaving through the narrow opening of the gate. A Plexiglas windscreen and helmet prevented her from seeing who was roaring past her car so quickly, almost catching the handlebars on her rental—*but she could guess.* Blondie was back!

Sophie turned to look over her shoulder, fumbling for her weapon.

The motorcycle skidded to a halt in front of Shank Miller, and the driver raised a weapon.

Miller stumbled back in surprise, his hands up. Sophie didn't wait to see what happened next. She threw the car into reverse and stomped on the gas.

The Neon shot backward, barreling in reverse down the driveway, and Sophie only had time to hope Miller would be smart enough to jump out of the way when her rental careened into the motorcycle with a shriek of rending metal.

Chapter Twenty-Five

The shock of the rental car's impact with the motorcycle was much more intense than Sophie had anticipated. Her body flew forward, hitting the airbag as it deployed so hard that her vision filled with colored lights even as her body whipped back again to hit the seat, her head connecting with the hard foam neck support. The airbag pinned her in place for an endless moment, muffling her panic in smothering whiteness.

Sophie batted at the poufy material and the thing deflated, settling around her like a discarded wedding gown. She dug her weapon out of the holster and got her door open, fighting her way out of the enveloping shroud of the airbag. Finally, free of it, she ran around the side of the car.

Shank Miller was flat on his back, several feet from the motorcycle, his eyes closed.

The motorcycle, crunched beneath the car's bumper, had flung its rider several feet away. The attacker, medium-sized in black leather, had staggered upright and was reaching for the weapon that had fallen to the ground.

Sophie ran toward the leather-clad assailant, turning to spin into a sidekick that nailed the perp in the solar plexus. The invader flew backward, crashing to the ground. Sophie followed up, standing over the cyclist with her weapon drawn. "Don't even think of getting up."

Jake, Ronnie, and Jesse barreled out of the guesthouse.

"What the hell?" Jake yelled.

"Miller is down!" Sophie yelled. "Check him!"

Jake ran to the rocker and knelt beside the prone man. Sophie spared a glance to see Miller sitting up, groaning and twitching. "Oh my God, what the hell did he hit me with?" the rocker moaned.

"Taser." Jake detached the prongs leading from the center of Shank's shirt to the weapon on the ground. "Hurts like a bitch, but you'll be okay."

The figure on the ground was medium size, identity and gender obscured by the heavy leathers.

Sophie leaned down and unclipped the webbing strap of the mirrored helmet and pulled it off the perp's head.

Blue eyes in a square, pale face. Blond mullet plastered down with sweat. "I'll kill you, bitch!" said Bobby Miller.

The man's hand darted toward a knife at his hip. Quick as crushing a venomous snake, Sophie stomped on Bobby's arm with a booted foot. The snap of a bone breaking was almost as satisfying as the man's scream of frustrated rage.

Sophie reached down and drew the knife, holding it up. She turned to address Jake. "I don't think we will have trouble any longer with getting jail time for this man."

––––––

Restraining the hysterically enraged Bobby Miller, communicating with MPD, assisting Shank into the house and getting him checked out, and the ensuing interview with Detective Cruz all slowed Sophie down. She even had to call the car rental company and report the damage to her vehicle.

By then it was afternoon.

She still needed a car and didn't want to alert Jake to her plans, so she went into the kitchen. She found Antigua working some stretchy-looking dough with her strong, glossy arms.

"Thought I'd make a few homemade pizzas," the chef said. "Everyone seems to get hungry after a crisis."

"I've noticed that too." Sophie leaned on one of the counter stools and felt the aftermath of adrenaline threatening to swamp her. *She had to stay focused.* "My car is being towed by the rental company tomorrow morning and I still have to run an errand. Can I borrow something of Miller's?"

"Sure. Take the Honda CR-V in the garage—that's the estate's runaround car." Antigua's shoulders gleamed in the overhead light as the woman kneaded and stretched the dough. "That was amazing, what you did. The kitchen window over-looks the turnaround." She indicated the long, broad window facing the estate's driveway. "I saw the whole thing. You didn't even miss a beat. And even though that man's lawyer is making noise about his injury, I'm glad you broke his arm."

Sophie smiled. "You are fond of Mr. Miller. I find that I am, too. I thought whoever was on the motorcycle was going to shoot him, so—I was a little violent."

"You were badass!" Antigua's smile was admiring. "Wasn't she, Jake?"

Sophie turned to look at her partner as he entered the kitchen. "Sophie is the baddest badass." Jake said. His grin was as cocksure as ever, but it faded as they locked eyes.

Sophie could not look away. Her mouth dried. Her heart thudded. She felt dizzy, and wanted to throw herself on him and feel him crush her close.

What the hell was this? She must be in shock or something.

Jake swung abruptly toward the big steel fridge and reached inside for a beer. "Miller's in love with you, Soph. He told me he's drafting a marriage proposal."

"Ha," Sophie said. "Your joking makes me uncomfortable. I have told you this. Please stop."

"He really did say that. And I can't help myself, sometimes." Jake turned, popped the top, and took a long drink. Sophie tore her gaze away from the sight and kept her eyes on Antigua as the woman tossed the circle of dough in the air and caught it.

"I wouldn't blame Miller a bit if he was smitten." Antigua said. "Jake, I was just telling Sophie I saw the whole thing from the window—and what she did was like something out of a movie."

"Just doing my job. But I could use a beer, too, today." Something had to work to calm her abraded nerves, steady her for the job ahead.

Jake pulled out another beer, popped the top, and handed it to her. Something like electricity zapped her fingers as their hands touched, and she almost dropped the bottle. He moved away and leaned on the counter. "I thought you didn't like beer."

"Sometimes it's necessary." Sophie lifted the bottle, took a swig, and grimaced. "Unfortunately, it has not improved since the last time I tried it." She took another big sip, but she really didn't like the beverage. Two gulps were more than enough. She set the bottle on the counter. "Well, I have a quick errand to run. See you all soon."

"Keys are inside the garage on a peg," Antigua called. "Come back in time for pizza!"

"I would hate to miss it." *Perfectly true.* Sophie walked out, conscious of Jake's gaze on her back.

Hopefully this wouldn't be the last time she ever saw him.

Chapter Twenty-Six

The cheap motel across from the Paradise Treasures gallery building, whose room she'd secured online under her alias, at least had a functioning air conditioner. Afternoon in Lahaina was sweltering, and the little window unit squeaked and groaned, dripping audibly as Sophie set up her surveillance station.

She checked all the windows facing the gallery building. She'd done a search and confirmed that the gallery rented not just the bottom floor, but all six floors of the building, two floors of which were given over to residential units.

Assan was in one of them. She was certain of it. The six-floor building had a great vantage point of the parking lot where they'd been shot at by the drone. He'd probably watched from one of the units and operated the drone from there, safe and comfortable. No wonder the police hadn't been able to find anyone in the street who might have been operating the unit.

Sophie had expected no less.

Assan might be on the other side of the building, but it was too late to change her position. She just had to hope that she'd spot him. Sophie took the TV off the peeling wooden laminate stand and pushed the stand over to the window. She unfolded a tripod and positioned it on the stand in front of the window, mounting a powerful pair of binoculars on it. Now that she'd made her escape from the Miller estate and was safely ensconced here, she had all the time in the world to stalk her prey.

She took her time going over the weapons, loading them, adjusting the holsters, and giving each a rubdown before she finally set her eyes to the binoculars, leaning over to stretch her back, scanning across the building. Her visual field took in the whole of the building, the street in front, and the small parking lot to the rear.

The smell of gun oil, the cool breeze from the humming air conditioner, and the stressful multitude of decisions she had made that had led to this moment—all of it fell away as Sophie blocked out sound with her headphones and settled in to wait, working a slow grid across the front of the sixth floor, searching.

She had to stop Assan. Connor had failed to do so, and had lost his life. The FBI had had its chance to deal with her ex.

She tracked slowly, letting breathing relax her into a hypnotic state.

From her position, she covered both the front and the back entrances to the gallery. After ascertaining that all the windows of the upper two floors were closed and covered by blinds, Sophie redirected her surveillance to the entrance and exits of the gallery.

She spotted Magda Kennedy pulling into a reserved spot near the gallery's back door in a sleek silver Mercedes coupe. The woman opened her door and got out. Even in the binoculars' ruthlessly magnifying eye, Kennedy looked stunning. Not a hair of her shining black coif was out of place as she retrieved a briefcase from her seat. She must not be working the floor today, because she wore an ivory silk blouse and a black pencil skirt with high heels. The woman hit the lock button, making the car's lights flash, then swiped a keycard over the back door and disappeared inside.

So, Kennedy didn't live on the premises. *Who occupied those top floors?* Were they rentals?

Sophie pushed away from the binoculars. Her eyes needed a rest, and this clearly was going to take a while. She pulled a small digital video camera out of her backpack and aimed it at the exit—if Assan left the building, it wasn't going to be through the highly visible front gallery area.

She set the recorder to feed to her phone and then opened her satellite link laptop, doing a search for the TMK number of the Paradise Treasures building.

The fifth floor was broken into three units, all rented. The sixth floor was one large unit, listed as "storage."

"Storage, my left buttock," Sophie muttered. The top floor sported a balcony with a round table and a couple of lounge chairs, clearly visible. She applied her eyes to the binoculars and investigated the area carefully. A sliding glass door granted egress to the deck, and closed blinds hid whoever or whatever was contained by the apartment—but there was no way that penthouse just held art and framing materials.

Sophie picked up her phone, eyeing the list of missed calls, wishing she hadn't given any of her friends or her father Mary Watson's number. Right on cue, the phone vibrated again—*Jake.*

Sophie suppressed a pang of guilt and slid the phone under the thin pillow to muffle it. She reapplied her eye to the lenses, moving to check each person who went in or out of the building.

She had swiped a bag of nuts and nibbled on some, wishing she'd taken longer to provision herself for this stakeout. She'd been in too much of a hurry to get out of Miller's compound and get set up—but now that she was, the biggest danger lay in breaking cover and drawing attention to herself.

The sunset over Lahaina was a long pageant, beginning with a golden glow and ending with spectacular, salmon-streaked clouds over the low violet silhouette of Lanai on the horizon. Sophie wished she could enjoy it, but every hour that went by narrowed the window of possible discovery. Jake would sound the alarm soon, and eventually, Miller's CR-V, abandoned several blocks away, would be discovered. Her partner would likely guess what she was up to and look for places where she might have been able to rent a room, or assume she'd been taken by Assan. Neither option was good.

Lights bloomed on in the sixth floor of the building, and Sophie's pulse picked up. A man's burly shadow passed across drapes lit from within.

Assan was there.

But she had no way to confirm her intuition.

The gallery closed. Streetlights came on. Magda Kennedy exited through the back door, tossed a briefcase into the Mercedes, fired it up, and left.

If Sophie'd been able to get into the Ghost software, she was almost sure that program could have hacked the building's security and reset it. Hours had gone by, and Sophie still didn't have full confirmation of Assan's presence.

But he was in that building. On the sixth floor. And he was too smart to show himself.

"Snake demon with a forked tongue," Sophie snarled. She pushed away and dropped to the floor to do pushups.

A hundred later, her energy coming back, Sophie stood and went through a quick version of her cardio and yoga program, ending seated in lotus position, calm and clear.

Time to get this done.

Chapter Twenty-Seven

Sophie took a quick shower to further clear her head. After dressing, she strapped on weapons at shoulder, hip, and ankle, slipping a slender knife into a flat Velcro scabbard on her calf. She slid on a black cotton pocketed vest to hide all of the weapons. She packed her small backpack and wiped down the weapons and all the surfaces of the room. Putting on one of Shank Miller's logoed trucker hats with Mary Watson's big sunglasses, Sophie checked around the area for any signs of personal occupation.

She'd removed everything.

Sophie left the motel without speaking to anyone. Sunset had finally yielded to velvety night, but streetlights shed bright yellow pools of light on the sidewalks where people still passed to and fro, their voices bright, preoccupied with their Maui vacation and happy feelings that Sophie could scarcely remember.

She crossed the street, checking that the area was clear. She stowed her backpack in a dark area behind one of the dumpsters and stayed in the deepest shadows as she slid along the back of the Paradise Treasures Gallery.

Coming from behind, she hit the surveillance camera covering the back door with a shot of matte black paint. Dropping to a squat, she took out a tiny set of Phillips-head screwdrivers and, working quickly, unscrewed the keycard slider mechanism, lowering it to dangle from one wire. She disconnected the card reader contacts and brushed them against each other. A spark lit the dark, and the back door gave an accommodating click.

Rising, Sophie quickly replaced the broken keycard mechanism so it wouldn't draw attention, and grasped the handle of the door in her gloved hand, pushing it down. The door yawned open, revealing a dark hall. Sophie slipped inside and shut the door.

The break-in hadn't taken more than two minutes.

She turned to the panel beside the back door, looking for the alarm. Sure enough, a timer was already counting down, activated by the door opening. *She had three minutes to find the code.*

Sophie sprayed the buttons on the panel with a fluorescing spray and hit the pad with a handheld black light. Four numbers, smudgy with fingertip grease, lit up. She plugged the four numbers into her phone's codebreaker software, and ran the combinations.

She punched them in. Five seconds showed on the timer when the alarm went green.

Sophie let out her breath in relief, stowed her tools, and walked down the hall. She tested the doors along the hallway, checking for anyone still in the building. They were all locked.

Sophie scanned for the elevator. She looked for cameras and saw none in this back area—*but that didn't mean she wasn't being watched.*

Sophie found the elevator, hidden behind a painted screen, near the service counter where she'd picked up her painting. But did she want to take it, and possibly alert anyone left in the building by the mechanical sounds it made, the lights changing?

There had to be a set of stairs.

The stairs were back behind a decorative column, and they were locked. Sophie took out her lock picks and went to work.

She opened the stairwell door cautiously and peeked up from beneath her billed cap. A surveillance cam in a dome-shaped covering eyed her with its blank stare. She tipped her head down, took aim at the dome, and shot it with the black paint. The stairwell filled with the sharp smell of the paint.

In case she'd missed something, Sophie kept back against the wall and ascended the stairs on light feet, her weapon drawn.

She was not going to be caught by surprise again.

Reaching the top of the stairs, she tried the handle of the door marked 6.

The knob turned with the well-oiled ease of a good piece of hardware; much better quality than the one below—which was odd.

She frowned, looking down at the matte steel handle in her gloved hand. This door lock would have been much more challenging for her to pick than the first one—the mechanism was heavy, the brand name expensive. *And yet, it was open.*

But she'd come this far. She had to check what, or who, was on this floor.

She turned the handle and gave a gentle pull.

The door swung soundlessly open to reveal a foyer-like area. A lacquered black door, framed by waist-high Chinese dragons in brass, stood directly ahead of her. The setup reminded her of her father's apartment in Nuʻuanu on Oahu: tasteful. Expensive. Apparently empty, but very secure.

Sophie hesitated in the doorway.

If Assan was there, he had to know she was coming.

As if responding to her thoughts, the shiny door opened.

"Hello, Sophie." Assan spoke casually, confidently, dark eyes beneath heavy brows sliding over her like greasy fingers. He was dressed in a black silk martial arts *gi* over matching pants, a cruel smile bending his full mouth. "You took your time getting here."

Sophie's heart beat with heavy thuds. She raised her weapon

and pointed it at the middle of his chest. "Today is a good day to die."

Chapter Twenty-Eight

Assan laughed. "You want to kill me so soon? That's no fun at all."

Of all the things Sophie had imagined, this was not one of them—Assan waiting for her, greeting her, unarmed, apparently nonchalant. He wasn't afraid of her. He hadn't been that last time either, when she'd almost shot him.

He didn't know how much she'd changed from the cowed young bride she'd been.

"I wonder how you'll explain away murdering an unarmed man. That won't do your career in security much good," Assan said.

"I don't care how it looks." *It wasn't murder when the person was already trying to kill you.* "Do you want it in the head, or the heart?" This had to be done, not just for revenge, but for the good of humanity. She understood the Ghost's mindset more every day.

"You must be hungry, thirsty. That stakeout across the street seemed a little unplanned. Come in, I've prepared some refreshments for us." Assan pushed the door wider. "You can check for threats, if you like."

"You are a threat just by breathing."

"You overestimate me." He leered. "I made a permanent impression on you and loom large in your life. They say your first always does."

This was the man who'd stolen her innocence and tortured her in ways she didn't even want to remember. How he'd enjoyed it! *And she wasn't his only victim.*

"I know what you are, now." Sophie took a step out of the stairs' doorway. "A sadist who preys on the fear and suffering of others. A conscienceless psychopath, a disease on the earth that needs to be stamped out. Thanks for making it easy for me." Eyes on Assan, she advanced slowly, peripheral vision alert. Assan liked to do his own dirty work, but he was no purist. He'd have a backup plan or other staff handy if he needed them.

"You want revenge. I understand that. But if you shoot me —someone you care about will suffer. Someone who needs you to let her out of a very dark place." He held up his phone. On it, too far away to make out, she could see a live video feed with a human figure against some kind of white backdrop.

Sophie halted. The Glock felt too heavy for her hands.

Of course, he wasn't just going to let her come in and shoot him. He'd anticipated her moves, watched her, and found leverage to use against her. This was Assan, and that was how he operated. She had to find whoever it was, get that person out, *then* shoot him.

Her phone was on in the small webbing athletic pack around her waist. She needed help. She lowered the weapon and pointed it at his groin. "I don't need to kill you right away. We can take it in stages."

Assan chuckled richly. "How my child bride has grown up. I've never found anyone quite like you, which is why I've gone to all this trouble to get you back. You're mine, you know. No one else will ever put his hands on you. I've made sure of that."

Sophie took another step forward. "What do you mean?" Connor's face rose in her mind's eye. *This was her chance to find out if Assan had anything to do with his death.*

"There will never be anyone but me, for you." He spoke the same words Connor had written Sophie in his note, and though she shuddered, *it wasn't a straight answer*. Assan opened his arm in a welcoming gesture. "I've taken care of your lovers and made sure that there will never be anyone else for you, either. And in the end, you came to me just as I planned."

Sophie needed more information before she shot him. *But like she'd told him, they could take it in stages.* She lowered the pistol to point at his knee.

"No, no, no." Assan held up the phone again. "You shoot me, and I push this button. The air keeping the woman you need to rescue will be cut off."

Sophie swallowed a ball of tightness, of hatred, of helpless frustration. "What do you want?"

"You, of course. Come in. Relax. I'm no barbarian. We can have a drink."

A sense of hopelessness rose in Sophie, swamping her like a rising tide.

Inevitable.

Her capture, her suffering, her death at his hands—already scripted. She couldn't catch a break to save her life—a cliché Jake had said one time about a hapless co-worker.

Jake.

She had to get word to him. Marcella was too far away to help.

Sophie lowered the weapon to block her action as she slipped a hand into the waist pack, pressing hard on Jake's number, speed dial number one on the burner phone. She felt the vibration of the phone. "Where is this woman you're holding captive?"

Sophie heard a faint squawk from the phone. *He'd picked up.* She just had to keep the line open so he could track her. She walked into the apartment, and the door swung shut behind her.

"She's somewhere safe. We're in no hurry. A few hours more or less won't make a difference to her—as long as she's breathing." Assan preceded Sophie into a spacious, luxuriously appointed living area. He gestured to a round, lacquered table set for two, glasses at each place. "Water and wine."

Sophie shook her head. "Do you really think we can sit down together while you hold a woman's life in your hands as leverage over me? Do you think this will solve anything? I will still hate you."

Assan's dark eyes glittered. "It is perfectly acceptable that you hate me."

A chill passed over Sophie. Yes, he still enjoyed every moment of her torment; it was an aphrodisiac to him. *Indifference was the answer.*

She shrugged. "Very well. Let's get this over with. Whatever this is." She sat down. "But you can taste my beverages first, if you don't mind."

"Clever girl." Assan reached over and sipped her water glass, quaffed her wine. "Your weapons, please. All of them."

Sophie looked at the phone in his hand, at the woman's figure, bound, dimly lit, twisting on a bed. She looked at the circular red button on the surveillance app that controlled his prisoner's air supply. This woman could be anywhere in the world! She couldn't take that chance right now. *She'd have to find another way to kill him.*

Every movement heavy and slow, Sophie took her Glock out of the shoulder holster and the second .19 out of the hip holster and set the guns on the table.

"Your ankle piece." Assan gestured with his wine glass. "And that waist pack."

She had to work in a location for Jake to come find her. She glanced around the apartment with its stunning art on the walls. She leaned down, removing the small Colt six shot she kept in an ankle holster. "Paradise Treasures is full of surprises. The sixth floor is listed as 'storage,' you know. Magda Kennedy has you stashed up here like a mad old relative that must be hidden."

Assan's mouth tightened in annoyance. He slipped into Mandarin. "Like your mother?"

Sophie's breath hissed out. *He was so good at this.* She answered in the same language. "Yes. Like my mother, poor sad woman that she is."

"You're becoming like her with time."

Had he found her Mary Watson apartment, seen her drop down the well of her depression after Connor's death? Had he hacked into the Security Solutions AI feed? *Probably.* It was safer to assume that he knew everything.

Sophie took off the waist pack and its precious tools, set it on the table with the rest. "That's everything, you bastard." She glared at him, shoving the pile of weapons toward him. "I don't need any of these things to kill you." She picked up the glass, careful to sip from a side of it that hadn't touched his mouth.

"You'll pardon me if I don't take your word for it. Stand up."

Hopefully Jake had heard her location and was on his way. She stood and Assan frisked her, sliding his hand over her hips, down her legs, between them, slow and lascivious, trailing his fingers over her thighs and butt. Sophie stared straight ahead. The slender, razor sharp knife was still strapped to her calf in the flat Velcro holder that was designed to fool pat-downs, and she let out a held breath as he moved on, going into the kitchen. "You need something to eat. You're getting too thin, stringy as an old chicken." The kitchen's sleek steel expanse of cabinetry and built-in appliances looked barely used. Assan opened the refrigerator, producing a wrapped tray. "You used to like sushi."

Sophie's belly tightened. She *was* hungry, but accepting food from him was giving ground. "You haven't told me what you require to let your prisoner go."

"Twenty-four hours. I require your complete cooperation and submission to me for twenty-four hours." Assan smiled. Vultures had more warmth in their eyes.

"No." Sweat broke out under Sophie's arms. "I will kill you first, or die trying."

He set the tray of sushi on the table and held up the phone. "This woman means something to you, does she not?" He hit a button. Lights came on in the video feed.

Sophie leaned forward to peer at the phone.

Her friend, Lei Texeira, lay on a king-sized bed in nothing but bra and panties, her hands and feet bound behind her back. She was blindfolded and gagged with a rubber ball, and in response to the lights, she thrashed uselessly on the bed. Her skin looked bleached in the video, her hair a tangled, curly brown nimbus against the pale sheets.

"No," Sophie whispered. "Oh no." *Her dear friend had already been through so much!* "Let her go. She's a mother! She has a child who needs her!"

"She's a cop. And I don't like cops." Assan extinguished the lights with a satisfied punch of his finger. "But I will let her go. Once I've had your complete submission for twenty-four hours."

Chapter Twenty-Nine

Sophie ate the sushi. She drank the water and refused the wine. She needed strength for what lay ahead.

Assan unzipped her waist pack to reveal her lock picks, small electrical toolkit, tape, and phone. "Ah. Likely you tried to call someone. Unfortunately for you, I have a jammer inside this apartment." Hope of rescue died as Assan picked up Sophie's Glock and brought the gun's butt down hard on the phone, smashing it. "Come. We have places to go."

Sophie schooled her face into that mask he'd taught her so long ago, standing silently. He walked around the table, drawing a hand down her cheek. "This scar. You're so ugly, now."

She swung her head and snapped her teeth at his hand, almost catching his fingers. He laughed, lifting the phone in his other hand.

"Submission, my dear. That was the agreement. When you don't cooperate, your friend suffers." He pushed another of the row of buttons on the side of the video app. The image of Lei convulsed abruptly, arching and shuddering on the bed in trembling, agonized spasms.

"Electrodes. On very sensitive parts of her anatomy." Assan's eyes gleamed. "I enjoyed taping them on."

"Oh God, no," Sophie whispered. "Stop. Make it stop." She could take any amount of pain herself, but not that inflicted on someone she loved. *How had he learned that?* "Please make it stop."

Assan pushed the button again and the body of her friend went limp. "I like it when you beg." He snaked out an arm to grab Sophie by the back of the neck, hauling her in to kiss her brutally with teeth, tongue, and violence.

Sophie shut her eyes and detached.

Assan let go eventually, and Sophie cast her eyes down so he wouldn't see the rage—it would only arouse him more. He stroked her cheek again. "Better. Now follow me."

Assan turned and walked out of the apartment, so confident that she was cowed and neutralized that he gave her his back. Sophie walked after him, spitting his foul taste from her mouth. Could she bend and get the knife up and into him before he had time to punch the button on the phone?

Unlikely. She'd have to kill him instantly, and he was on alert, the phone in his hand. She had to bide her time, wait for a moment when his hands were occupied or he was distracted.

He led her to the elevator and pushed an unmarked button. "You are right to conclude that Paradise Treasures is full of surprises. There's another floor down below the building."

The doors closed. The elevator shot downward as Assan turned to fondle her, sliding his hands over her breasts and down her abs, holding the phone up to taunt her with her helplessness.

Sophie kept her eyes open, watching for his distraction.

Her body was just a thing now, an object to be touched, used, abused, and discarded—by herself as much as him, as she abandoned her physical self to focus on getting that phone away.

Assan pinched and twisted her nipples, bringing involuntary

tears to her eyes. Every wince and gasp made him more aroused, and he slid a hand down to grasp her sex, staring into her eyes, grinding against her, refusing to let her withdraw.

Sophie looked right back. She rehearsed killing him: *the bulge of his features as she strangled him, the pulsing jet of his blood as she stabbed him and cut an artery, the bursting of his intestines as she gutted him…*

"You hate me so much," he breathed into her ear, licking her neck. "It makes me hot."

The tiny ding of the elevator's halt hardly seemed to register to Assan as he pushed her against the wall, panting, raping her with his hand and the pressure of his body, a preview of what was coming next.

The elevator door opened. The phone lowered as he turned —and Sophie whipped her knee up, knocking the phone out of his hand. The device landed on the floor of the elevator, and she kicked it with her other foot so that it flew out into the hall.

The doors began closing automatically as Assan stumbled after the phone with a curse.

Sophie bent, whipped up her pant leg and pulled out the slender blade. She coiled and sprang, landing on Assan's back, knocking him flat to the floor. Her knee in his spine, she grabbed his hair and yanked his head back, setting the point of the knife against his throat. "Where is she?"

He held up his hand with the phone in it.

"Where is she? Tell me now and I won't kill you." Sophie's mouth had gone so dry that she could hardly force the words out.

"She's dead. You brought this on her." Assan whispered hoarsely. "I'll never tell you where she is."

He'd had a chance to bargain for his life.

He was never going to let either of them go.

"Wrong answer." Sophie buried the knife in Assan's throat, feeling nothing but determination to finish the grim task. Even with the wickedly sharp edge of the blade, cutting through the sinew and corded muscle of his neck took surprising effort, and he bucked spasmodically, trying to dislodge her, thrashing like a landed marlin between her thighs. The sharp reek of the hot blood jetting from his neck filled her nostrils and she shut her eyes and held her breath, waiting.

A seemingly endless moment later, Sophie dropped Assan's head into the spreading pool of blood and retrieved the phone from his clenched hand.

The device was black, the screen locked down. Assan was still dying, messy gurgles and spasms racking his body, as she grabbed his hand and pressed his forefinger down on the phone's activation button, hoping it was set to his fingerprint.

The phone bloomed into life on the familiar scene of Lei on the bed, and Sophie stood up, resetting the phone's security quickly to keep the screen open, then switching back to the video.

The red button now showed as a black X.

Assan had cut off Lei's air.

"Poxy swine!" Sophie kicked the still-twitching body. "If I could kill you again I would!"

Assan went still at last.

Sophie looked down the hallway into the bowels of the basement beneath the building, desperation tightening her throat. She wiped the knife on her pants and stowed it in the holster on her leg, forcing her mind to work. *If she'd had her computer rigs or even her own phone, she could try to track the signal that his phone was picking up.* But even if she had been able to hack his phone's signal to track the video, it would only identify the address, not exactly where in the building the signal was originating from.

She didn't know where Lei was, but chances were good she was on this floor somewhere—he'd brought Sophie down here for a reason. She'd try all the doors on this level first.

Sophie tried the phone to call Jake. "No signal. *Dung of a four-horned goat!"*

She bent and rifled through Assan's pockets and pulled out a key ring with a grunt of satisfaction, straightening to run forward down the dimly lit hallway.

Chapter Thirty

Sophie's gloved hands were sticky with Assan's blood as she reached for the first door handle—*locked, of course.* She flipped through the keys, her hands trembling with urgency. *Car key, a couple of room keys, a small one that looked like it went to a security box…* She pushed the others aside and just tried the room keys.

Neither fit.

She worked her way down the hall, stuffing her panic somewhere down deep where it could be used as fuel for action. *Feelings didn't help. Compartmentalizing did.*

None of the room keys worked. She ended up back at the bloody mess that was the remains of her ex.

"Why did you bring me down here?" She yelled at the body, giving in to the urge to kick him again. *"Damn you to hell where you're no doubt burning!"*

How much time did Lei have?

There was no way to know. If she was just in a sealed room, she might be okay for a while. Sophie had to hope—and she had to get help.

She got on the elevator and punched the button back up to the penthouse. Outside Assan's apartment, she tried for a signal again and was able to get a call through to Jake, though he didn't pick up. "This is Sophie. I'm at the Paradise Treasures Gallery on the sixth floor." She swallowed. "Assan has Lei Texeira hidden somewhere and her air supply has been cut off. I need help locating her! Call me back at this number."

She hung up with a punch of the button. She should call 911, but when they found Assan's body, wouldn't they just arrest her? No. She needed someone from MPD who knew her, and would be able to help her navigate this messy crisis. She could call Stevens, Lei's husband—but she needed someone whose judgment wouldn't be clouded by emotion.

Pono, Lei's partner.

She called MPD and asked for Detective Kaihale. When told he was away from his desk, she got assertive. "This is regarding his partner Lei Texeira's safety. He is going to want to speak to me." She left the number of Assan's cell. Contacting people was remarkably difficult without her own phone and list of saved private numbers.

She needed to find a way to access her own programs and hack the phone's video signal while she waited for backup.

Sophie searched Assan's work area, locating the jamming device behind his computer and deactivating it. Sitting down at his computer, she was faced with his password protection and none of her own handy software to circumvent it.

She typed in his former code, his birthdate, their address in Hong Kong—and couldn't believe her luck when their anniversary date unlocked his screen.

Sophie hopped onto his hard drive and scanned for video programs, locating a hosting site that was downloaded. She accessed the Cloud and her store of tech, sending a backtrace to comb through the videos—and it didn't take long to twig to the live feed of Lei.

The room was dark but for the thin green glow of some nightlight illumination set to monitor her. Sophie hit the lights app on the phone to see if Lei responded, and the screen bloomed into brightness.

Her friend was lying quietly on her side, and this time did not struggle and thrash in response to the light. Sophie zoomed in, and could see Lei's abdomen moving as she breathed.

Her friend was still alive!

Sophie deployed backtrace software to yield a location of the origin of the video stream.

At least, she could be certain what building Lei was in! She needed to call Michael Stevens, Lei's husband. A lieutenant at MPD, he'd have resources and be highly motivated to help.

She did a quick online search for his private cell number, and with access to her more high-tech tools, was able to find it.

Thankfully, he answered an unknown number calling, his baritone voice terse. "This is Stevens."

"Michael, it's Sophie. I have bad news and I need your help."

A beat. "What is it? Is it Lei? She was supposed to be home hours ago."

"Yes. She's been kidnapped by Assan Ang and is...somewhere. I'm trying to locate her exact position. I called Pono, but he didn't pick up. You should call this in to MPD and bring backup to my location. Hopefully by the time you get here, I will have found her."

Oh, how she hoped so.

Sophie rattled off the address of Paradise Treasures and hung up before he could ask her anything more.

As she calmed from that ordeal, she considered.

What had Assan taken her down to the basement for, if none of the keys opened the doors down there?

Perhaps she'd missed something on his body. She hadn't wanted to spend any longer touching him than strictly necessary...

The phone buzzed. Sophie recognized Jake's number and picked up.

"Good God, woman! You scared the pants off me. I'm outside Paradise Treasures and it looks shut up tight."

"It isn't. Hit the back door and come up here. I'm trying to find Lei Texeira. Assan's got her stashed somewhere, and I'm afraid she's going to suffocate."

"On my way." He ended the call.

Sophie whooshed out a breath of relief. *She wasn't alone in this.* She took a moment to wash the blood off her gloved hands at the apartment's sink.

The backtrace dinged with a location just as Jake flung open the apartment's door. "What the hell is going on?"

"I don't have time for that now," Sophie leaned in to pull up the data. She imported it into another search tool. "Lei's in this building somewhere," Sophie confirmed, and shot to her feet. "I have to go back down and search Assan's body again."

"His body?" Jake put a hand out to stop her. "Wait. Slow down."

"I can't! Lei might not have much air left. Follow me." She handed Jake the phone with Lei showing in the video feed, pushing past him toward the elevator.

"Shit." Jake followed, looking at the phone, as she stabbed the button. "What's going on?"

"I killed Assan in the basement. Slit his throat."

"Fuck me—really?" Jake's voice was faint. Sophie glanced at him as he scrubbed a hand over his face. "You need a lawyer."

"Indeed. But I'm the one who was almost fucked, and still might be if I can't find Lei in time." Sophie sketched out events briefly as the elevator hummed downward through the floors. "I don't know how much air she has left. But at least she's in this building, for sure. I already checked all the doors down in the basement, but I must have missed something. Assan took me down there for a reason."

"Maybe he's got a hidden room or something."

"Exactly."

The elevator dinged, and opened to the sight of Assan's sprawled body, surrounded by a lake of congealing blood.

"Damn, Sophie."

"Yes, I believe I'm damned. Always have been. Nothing ever works out for me." Sophie was hardly aware of verbalizing her thoughts as she moved to the body. She patted Assan down more carefully. "I have to flip him."

Jake took hold of Assan's shoulder and helped roll him on his back. Blood had soaked the entire front of his shirt and down the man's pants, deeply saturating the material. Sophie kept her eyes off the massive grinning slash in his neck, feeling around his waist. "His belt. It's thicker than it should be." She pulled the belt out through the belt loops and handed it to Jake without looking at it, continuing to search the body. "Here." She fished a chain out from inside his shirt and yanked hard to break it, holding up the key dangling from it in a bloody gloved hand. She wiped the key off on her pants leg and ran forward into the hall, shoving it frantically into the sturdy deadbolt locks.

The third door opened.

Sophie sucked in a breath as she hit the lights.

Stark white walls, and a bed. A closed armoire on one wall. A screen with a sink and toilet behind it. And directly behind the bed, a massive wheel dangling with restraints, straps and irons.

"I'm guessing this is what he brought you down for." Jake's voice was somber.

"But where's Lei? Why isn't she in here?"

"Maybe he never intended to let her go. Or maybe there's a second room."

"Yes." Sophie lunged across the room to grab the armoire. "Help me!"

She and Jake shoved the cabinet away. Hidden behind it, a narrow outline marked the edge of a doorway flush with the wall. No handle marred the surface. Sophie leaned in, frantic, tracing along the edge of the opening, her gloves leaving smears of blood on the stark white wall.

"It must be a pressure lock," Jake said. "Push along the edge. He had to be able to open it somehow."

Working in tandem, they pushed and pressed around the door. Sophie heard a click, and the panel bumped out from the frame. She grasped the door and pulled it wide.

The room beyond was pitch black. She felt along the wall inside the door. *No light switch.*

Sophie fumbled Assan's phone out of her pocket and hit the lights app on the video feed.

Illumination bloomed brightly, revealing a tiny cubicle. A nightmare scene met her eyes: her friend Lei, motionless on a bed that almost filled the space. Lei was bound, blindfolded, and gagged, her tawny skin and dark, tangled hair a stark contrast to the whiteness of the sheets.

"Lei!" Sophie rushed to her friend's side, feeling for a pulse in her friend's neck.

Lei lashed out instantly with her legs, catching Sophie painfully in the side. Sophie leapt back as Lei continued to kick and struggle, clearly far from dead. Quick tears of relief filled Sophie's eyes as she spotted the orange dots of earplugs in Lei's ears, as well as the blindfold and gag—*her friend didn't know that she was being rescued!*

"Keep talking to her. I'll hold her feet," Jake grasped Lei's ankles.

Sophie leaned in to hold her friend's shoulders. "Lei! It's Sophie! We're here to get you out!"

Her friend's struggling subsided abruptly.

Sophie plucked the earplugs out of Lei's ears and lifted the blindfold. Lei blinked red-rimmed eyes. She spat out the rubber gag ball with a curse as Sophie loosened the strap behind her head. "Where's that son of a bitch? I'll kill him!"

"I got him first." Sophie sank onto the bed to draw her friend into her arms in a long hug as Lei shook and trembled with shock. Jake pulled a combat blade from a holster at his waist and slashed the duct tape holding Lei's feet together and arms behind her back.

Lei groaned as circulation rushed back into her limbs. "He grabbed me right outside the police station. I wasn't paying attention, just heading to my car." She shook her head. "The boldness took me by surprise, I'm embarrassed to say. The guy was dark-haired, with a thick stocky build. Six foot or so in height. He hit me with a Taser and threw me in a van. I woke up here, totally in the dark, all my senses shut down." She shuddered. "Gonna need some therapy after this adventure."

Sophie searched her friend's body for the electrodes and identified them, taped onto Lei's nipples beneath her bra and between her legs. "Can you get those off? Or do you want help?"

"I can do it. Just give me a minute. And some privacy." Lei shot a glance at Jake.

Jake stood up and turned away. "I'll step outside and make sure first responders are on the way."

"Yes, I called Lei's husband. Hopefully he'll be here shortly with backup," Sophie said. "Listen out for them."

Sophie turned back to Lei and chafed her hands and arms as Jake exited. "Leave the electrode tape where it is so the CSIs can see. Did anything else happen? Did he—rape you?" Her skin went hot and cold with horror at the thought.

"No, I'm okay," Lei said. "And of course, I'll leave the evidence in place." Her hands still trembled, tracing the wires to their taped-on nodes.

"Your attacker was my ex, Assan. He was using you as leverage to control me." Sophie bit her lip. "I'm sorry I brought this down on you. But it's over now. Permanently."

"Good. About time that dog was put down." Lei plucked the wires off the taped nodes gingerly as Sophie removed the small, remote-controlled power pack that had provided the shocks from beneath Lei.

"He said he had a control to cut off your air. Did you have any trouble breathing?" Sophie asked.

"No, I was okay for air. I think."

Sophie frowned, beginning to scan the room for any devices positioned near ventilation openings.

Michael Stevens, Lei's husband, filled the doorway. His dark brown hair was mussed, his blue eyes blazing. Sophie stood up and moved away as the lieutenant rushed in. "Sweets! I was just getting ready to call this in when Sophie got ahold of me. Where are you hurt?"

"I'm okay." Tears welled in Lei's eyes as Stevens gathered her up, his long arms winding around Sophie's friend's body and pressing her in close, his tousled head bending to kiss her. They rocked together for a long moment, murmuring incoherently, heedless of anyone who might see their passion.

Watching their reunion stabbed Sophie with grief. *With Connor gone, would she ever be loved like that?* She'd only had a taste of such devotion. She moved to the doorway, re-entering the room they'd first come through.

Jake was talking to two officers and Lei's longtime partner, Pono. They all looked up at the sight of Sophie, and the expression on Pono's face made Sophie's chest constrict.

"I'm sure you have a lot of questions for me," Sophie said.

"Yes." Pono, his big square face grave, made a gesture to the hallway. "I called the crime scene tech and Dr. Gregory at the ME's office to examine the body. We have to take an official statement from you down at the station."

Chapter Thirty-One

The clock on the wall read eleven p.m. when Sophie sat down with her lawyer at a steel table in the interview room at Maui Police Department's Kahului station. Sitting on the wrong side of that table felt surreal to Sophie.

Pono, seated next to the station's commanding officer, Captain C. J. Omura, recited the Miranda and turned on the recording equipment. The FBI was also being piped in via Skype on an open laptop.

"My client has a well-established case against Assan Ang, currently on the FBI's most wanted list. This perpetrator has made multiple attempts on Sophie Ang's life." Sophie's lawyer, Davida Fuller, was an athletic blonde with well-developed biceps.

"We are aware of the case." Omura, immaculate in her tailored uniform and sleek hair, was all business. She was Lei and Michael's boss and also their friend, and Sophie had met the well-groomed Japanese woman in a social context previously. "This isn't a courtroom, Ms. Fuller. We'll lead this interview, thank you very much. Now, Ms. Ang. Why don't you tell us, in your own words, how events unfolded?"

Fuller turned to Sophie. "No comment. Let them make their case."

Sophie twisted her fingers in her lap, grateful she wasn't cuffed and under arrest for Assan's murder—*at least, not yet.* Her gaze found Pono's warm brown eyes, then Omura's cool stare. She looked at the laptop finally, and recognized the pixelated ice-blue gaze of her former boss, Special Agent in Charge Ben Waxman. "Hello, Sophie," he said, gently.

"Hello, Ben. My, how the mighty have fallen." Sophie didn't mean for her tone to sound so bitter. "I should never have left the FBI."

"And we certainly wish you hadn't. You are surrounded by friends here. Just tell us what happened."

"No," Fuller said, laying a restraining hand on Sophie's arm. "This is all being recorded, and who knows what the DA and the Hong Kong authorities will do?"

Sophie shrugged Fuller's hand off. "I hear your recommendation and I choose to share my version of events."

Sophie told how she'd picked up a confidential clue to Assan's whereabouts. "I should have shared that with Special Agent Marcella Scott, who gave me every opportunity to do so. But I suspected that Assan had killed the man I was dating, Todd Remarkian. Assan had also engineered the near-fatal beating of another man I cared about." She looked down at her twisted fingers and straightened them deliberately. "As the records show, I turned Assan Ang over to the authorities the last time he tried to kill me, and he escaped. I considered that the 'clue' I had to Paradise Treasures was a trap—but I just didn't trust anyone else to bring him in."

"What prompted you to break into Paradise Treasures?" Omura asked. "Your entry was illegal and resulted in destruction of property."

"I'm sorry about that, and will gladly pay any damages." Sophie blew out a breath. "I had visited the gallery twice, as Jake Dunn can corroborate. He came with me the second time.

Something was just…not right about the place, and the owner, Magda Kennedy. I couldn't tell you exactly what. Perhaps it was just her demeanor, and the fact that she seemed to have a possible relationship with organized crime. Sergeant Texeira told me that she'd been investigated before. In any case, after the armed drone came after Jake and me and no trace of an operator was found in the area, I became convinced that Assan was hiding in the building, or at least had some connection to it. The sixth floor was labeled "storage" on the building's specs, but looked residential from the outside. So, I surveilled the building and saw a shadow inside once darkness fell, matching Assan's height and build. I decided it was time to go investigate more closely." Sophie described the series of events. "Assan knew I was coming. He had lured me in, and when I got to the apartment where he was residing, he secured my 'submission' by showing me a live video feed confirming that he had kidnapped my friend, Lei Texeira, well known to all of us here."

Omura inclined her head. "We've had time to take Sergeant Texeira's statement." During the hours between Lei's dramatic rescue and when Davida Fuller arrived at the station to represent Sophie, they'd likely also spoken to Jake.

"Good." Sophie looked up. "Assan frisked me in the apartment, and removed my weapons, leveraging me by torturing Lei. I'm sure she described how he used electricity to shock her, and you saw the evidence of how he did it. He threatened her life."

Pono nodded. "She said that he told you that he was going to suffocate her."

"Yes." Sweat burst out on Sophie's body at the memory of her frantic search for Lei. "He had a button on the phone app that he said controlled her air supply. I hoped that if I got the phone away, I'd have time to force him to tell me where she was. When I kicked the phone out of his grasp as the elevator opened, I was then able to pull a concealed knife that he had missed in searching me, and threaten him with it, asking for

Lei's location. He refused to tell me anything, only that she would die. He would never let either of us go. So, I killed him."

Sophie's bald words fell like stones from her mouth to roll into the quiet, echoing room. *They sounded too harsh.* She expanded her reasoning. "Based on Assan's statements to me and his previous history, this was the end for me. Assan was going to torture and kill me, and most likely, Lei, as well. He was a conscienceless sadist. He had no reason to let either of us go."

"And yet, he had blindfolded Lei and even stopped her hearing. She had only a general description of her attacker," Omura said. "She could have been released with no real ability to identify him."

"But not me. Never me. The investigators saw the room he intended for me to occupy." Sophie swallowed, suppressing panic. She hadn't really thought she'd be under investigation for murder, when he'd so clearly planned to torture her! But only she and Assan really knew what lay between them, and only Sophie had seen the lust and deadly intent in his eyes. "And what you say may be true about Lei. Assan was very crafty. He would have wanted to have all options available to him, including releasing Lei as a bargaining chip. All I can tell you is that, in the moment that I held the knife to his throat, I knew that he despised me. He doubted my ability to follow through with my threat to his life. He had no intention of ever letting me leave that basement, except in a body bag—and he had anticipated all my moves and lured me in. I had to take advantage of my one opportunity to defend myself."

A long moment of silence followed. Sophie looked down at the table, reaching up to rub the scar on her cheekbone. *"So ugly, now."* Assan's voice reverberated in her mind.

He could still destroy her life, even in his death.

"My client was clearly acting in self-defense however it might have looked in the moment." Fuller said. "There is a well-established history of domestic violence and multiple murder and kidnap attempts upon Sophie by this man."

"We are just trying to establish the chain of events, Ms. Fuller. The DA will determine what, if any, charges are brought against Ms. Ang for the death of her ex-husband," Omura said.

"And the FBI regrets being unable to apprehend this man and spare everyone involved stress and heartache," Waxman said from the monitor. "Sergeant Texeira is our FBI liaison to Maui. We are grateful to you, Sophie, for getting her out in time. And we are glad you did what you had to, to survive."

Waxman's support was a balm, and Sophie smiled at her former boss.

Pono cleared his throat. "About that. The room where Lei was being held was sealed. She'd have eventually suffocated without the door being opened, though there was no device that we could find that changed the air circulation or connected to Ang's phone app. So, he was…taunting you with that. But if no one had found Sergeant Texeira, she would have died within hours."

A long pause as they all digested this.

"Here's the problem I'm having with this whole scenario," Omura finally said, steepling shiny red nails and leaning forward to make eye contact with Sophie. "Threats and coercion aside, Assan Ang was unarmed. You attacked him from behind and cut his throat. This killing looks a whole lot more like an execution than self-defense. What do you have to say to that?"

This time, when Davida Fuller's hand dropped to rest on Sophie's forearm in restraint, Sophie lowered her gaze to her hands in her lap and stayed silent.

"My client has made her statement. And now, unless you are going to bring charges and arrest her, we've had a long night and have a trauma counselor to speak with in the morning." Fuller stood up and straightened her sleeveless sheath dress. Her shoulder muscles gleamed like armor. "Let's go, Ms. Ang."

They left the interview room, and no one tried to stop them.

Chapter Thirty-Two

Several days later, Sophie followed VP of Operations Kendall Bix across the dewy lawn of the Honolulu Resting Place, a small, tasteful cemetery specializing in cremation. Sophie's chest ached and her eyes felt dry and hot, the pressure of tears pressing on the backs of them. She thought she'd cried all she was going to. Apparently not. *But maybe when Connor's memorial was over, she could begin to move on.*

A big sun hat shaded Sophie from having to look at anyone and one of Mary Watson's floral sundresses swished against her legs as she led Connor's Doberman toward the ceremony area. *Anubis had been closest to him of anyone.* The thought almost made the tears spill as the dog walked beside her in his stately way, ears pricked with curiosity, sun gilding his sleek coat. Ginger was with Sophie's father, Frank, at his apartment, not trusted to behave at such a dignified event.

Sophie recognized few but co-workers from Security Solutions in the small crowd. Marcella, who she hadn't spoken to since their tiff over the phone, gave her a small smile and finger wave, angling over to walk with her. Sophie released a breath—

her friend was there to support her on this tough day. *She'd been forgiven.*

Bix had put together the service, and questioned Sophie if she had any contacts to be invited—but Connor had no family that anyone could find to notify of his death. The dearth of anyone but professional contacts smote Sophie. If she died, at least her father would mourn.

Had his real name even been Connor? Had anything about him been real? *Maybe only the emotion she'd felt in his arms…*

Sophie tripped a little, her slingback heel catching on an uneven tuft of grass.

"Careful." A male voice. A hand at her elbow, steadying her. Anubis turned his head, jerked and let out a short, sharp whine.

Sophie didn't look up, just tweaked her arm away and tugged Anubis closer. The Doberman could appear threatening to strangers who got too close, and though he had never attacked anyone to Sophie's knowledge, Connor's funeral wasn't the place for a first time.

Sophie just didn't have the energy to be social, to exchange pleasantries or trite, meaningless expressions of sadness when her despair was too great even to verbalize.

They arrived at a large, circular concrete pad inlaid with a mosaic design featuring the symbols of many of the major religions. Densely planted royal palms surrounded the space, giving the area a feeling of a tropical room with the sky as a ceiling. A lava-stone crypt stood ajar to one side, lined with shelves holding ash containers. Connor's remains, in a brass urn, rested in the center of a mosaic mandala.

There were no chairs. *This was likely going to be a short service.* What was there to say, after all, about a man so young, so isolated and secretive? Sophie clenched Anubis's leash, the chain cutting into her palm.

The small, quiet group filed around the mosaic area, filling in a semi-circle, with Marcella on her left. Sophie felt Jake's presence loom up into her space, warm and intrusive, pushing

Marcella off to the side. He took her dangling hand in his, and squeezed it.

His solid physical presence felt like a boulder she could lean on. Sophie sighed and rested against him, inhaling his familiar scent. She hadn't seen him since the debacle in Lahaina. During the last few days' isolation at her father's apartment awaiting a decision on whether or not she'd be charged with Assan's murder, she'd wondered dimly where he was. She still hadn't gotten a new phone to replace the one Assan had smashed, hadn't had the strength to deal with the rigmarole of setting it up. Her father had fielded calls on the apartment's landline while she struggled with her depression—and mostly gave in to it. The past couple of days spent in her bed were a blur.

She had met with Dr. Kinoshita for a post-incident debrief and trauma counseling on Oahu late in the day after making her statement at MPD. Sitting in the psychologist's cool modern office at Security Solutions, Sophie felt disembodied, distanced from her surroundings—an observer. Getting out of bed that morning at her father's had been extremely difficult.

Kinoshita wore a mint-green sheath dress with a pearl choker. One side of her sleek bobbed hair was held back with a gold clip in the shape of a butterfly. "How are you doing, Sophie?"

"I feel like I might not really be here," Sophie said. "I'm having trouble today. My body doesn't feel real. Even when I pinch myself." Sophie did so, hard, and the twist of pain was like a dim, faraway sound heard through a fog. *Maybe enough pain would put her back in her body—that had worked in the past.* She should go to the gym for another round with that Tongan fighter.

The psychologist looked up from her notes, dark eyes sharp behind modish black reading glasses. "When did this feeling start?"

"Ever since I rescued Lei." *Two days.* Two days was all it had been since the events in the basement in Lahaina. Two days of a persistent sense of detachment, as if she were stuck in some kind of plastic bubble, and everything was simply too much effort.

Kinoshita told her about "depersonalization," and that it was a symptom of having experienced a severe trauma, or could be part of an overall anxiety or depression disorder. "I'm depressed," Sophie said, tired of hiding, of trying, of the never-ending effort of it all. "I think I need medication."

So now she was taking a little white pill in the mornings. Not that it had made a bit of difference, though Kinoshita said it would take a few weeks to feel any better…and here she was at Connor's memorial.

Sophie's feet were too far away and her hands too close. Her body felt like an ill-fitting dress, hot and pinched. Only Jake felt real in the whole tableau around her.

The officiant was a short, rotund mixed-Hawaiian man in a dark shirt and pants, draped in a *tapa*-cloth *kihei* robe. He picked up an *ipu* gourd and began a strong percussive beat, his voice rich with the vibrato characteristic of a Hawaiian chant.

The ancient words in a foreign tongue washed over Sophie. She shut her eyes, letting go of her thoughts, letting go of control. She was conscious only of Jake's hand holding hers, his shoulder under her cheek, the warm strength of Anubis leaning on her leg, and the knowledge of Marcella on the other side of Jake. Even in her weird detachment bubble, she was loved.

The thumping of the ipu and the alchemy of the chant allowed her mind to float free and remember Connor.

His easy smile, hiding a brilliant mind. His laughter and generosity. His wicked, wonderful genius. That incredible musical ability. His touch, lighting her up, healing her damaged heart.

That he was gone, when she'd finally opened that heart— such bitter sorrow she couldn't even really feel it.

"You okay?" Jake whispered, lifting the hat to speak into her ear.

She nodded, and the motion of her head caused the tears filling her eyes to spill down her cheeks.

The *kahu* ended the chant. He said a few words about the fleetingness of life and the building of legacy. Todd Colin Remarkian would be remembered for what he had built, for the fortune he had left to rescue shelters that would help so many neglected and abused animals. He would have done much more, but he'd been lost too soon.

They had no idea how much more.

What would happen to the balance of evil in the world, with the Ghost no longer there to even the odds? The heavy brick of the Ghost software remained tucked away in her rucksack like it was nothing special. She hadn't tried to unlock it since Maui.

Bix had asked her to say a few words, but Sophie had refused, sure she could not articulate anything meaningful for public consumption.

Sophie kept her eyes down as Bix addressed the group. "Todd was tireless in his efforts to bring security to our clients by helping make the world a safer place. He was instrumental in developing the first ever artificial intelligence home surveillance system. His contributions will live on and continue to affect the world through different applications for years to come. Here from abroad, to speak a few words about his longtime business partner and friend, is the co-founder of Security Solutions, Sheldon Hamilton."

Sophie went rigid with shock. *Sheldon Hamilton!*

And just that suddenly, she was fully alert, back in her body.

The man who'd steadied her by the elbow, the man standing quietly on the other side of Anubis on her right, moved forward.

That man was also the one whose death they were mourning.

And Sophie was the only one who knew it.

Sheldon Hamilton turned to face them in front of the brass urn, and opened his mouth to speak at his own funeral.

Chapter Thirty-Three

Connor/Todd/Sheldon's eyes were dark brown. He wore a white straw fedora that cast his features into shadow. Fashionable square-rimmed tortoiseshell glasses obscured the line of his brows, and a goatee changed his chin from the front. He'd even put on lifted shoes and altered his posture.

If she hadn't known him so well, she'd have been fooled like all the rest.

Sophie's mouth had gone completely dry, but her skin felt clammy, her extremities numb.

How had she forgotten about Sheldon Hamilton? When the bomb went off and Connor supposedly died, he should have been the first person for her to track down. Instead, she'd wasted time looking for Connor's blond Todd Remarkian identity.

The enormity of the betrayal drained the blood from her head. *How could he have let her grieve him?*

She swayed and must have made some sound, because Jake squeezed her hand, hard. She could hardly feel his grasp.

"Todd Remarkian was a bundle of contradictions," Sheldon Hamilton said. His voice was different than Connor's, deeper and rougher. Probably a tone-altering device hidden beneath his buttoned collar.

He'd told her once that the secret to disguise was that people saw what they expected to see—but a few key details went a long way.

Whatever this man had to say about the death of his own fake identity, she didn't want to hear. The hypocrisy was too much to bear.

"Here." Sophie thrust Anubis's leash into Jake's hand. "Give this dog to Sheldon, his rightful owner. I have to go. I'm not feeling well."

She spun and strode away across the grass, breaking into a jog at the edge of the ring of palms, covering her face as if overcome by emotion.

She *was* overcome by emotion!

Rage at her own stupidity: *she'd been so obtuse, blinded by grief that she'd forgotten all about the alter ego he'd already fooled her with once.* Rage at him: *how could he have watched her suffer as she had?* How could he not have given her even a clue in the letter he left her in the safe deposit box?

Her eyes burned. Her diaphragm stuttered with the effort to breathe as heat and cold chased over her skin. Only sheer reflex and the need to flee kept her moving.

Sophie reached the pearl-colored Lexus SUV her father had given her on graduation from the FBI. She hadn't bothered with the Mary Watson identity since she got back from Maui. Now that Assan Ang was dead, she'd thought the need for pretense was over. *But it would never be over.* Her life was one long pretense.

"Sophie!" Marcella had come after her.

Damn it!

Sophie beeped the car open.

Maybe she should have walked up and ripped the Ghost's beard off in front of everyone instead of running away. The man was slipperier than a barrel of eels, but he was standing there at his own funeral, vulnerable. He'd run to avoid the FBI's investigation, most likely. This was her moment to both even the score, and restore her friendship with Marcella.

She leaned her forehead on the door, the handle in her hand, debating. Even though Connor had hurt her, she felt horrible turning him in. *He had her guts in knots, the cobra-headed hyena!*

Her friend reached her. Marcella set her hand on Sophie's shoulder. "Are you all right?"

Sophie looked up. "No, I'm not. This is all too much."

"I have good news. Something to make you feel better. A witness has come forward on Maui."

This was so out of context that Sophie looked up to meet her friend's eyes. Marcella nodded. "Yes. We have a witness who has gone on record to say that he was tasked with disposing of a drone mechanism the day of the attack on you and Jake in Lahaina. The man he described matches Assan Ang. The witness works for Magda Kennedy, so Lei is excited that they might finally be able to make a case against the gallery owner, too. This will really strengthen the argument that you killed Assan in self-defense. I hope knowing this helps, a little bit."

The sympathy in her friend's eyes…

The vicarious suffering Marcella had gone through on Sophie's behalf, the stress, the days of caring for Sophie when she was in bed, grieving…*it was wrong.*

"That is good news." Sophie opened the car door and tossed the ridiculous hat she wore into the back seat. "But Marcella, I'm not sad. I'm furious."

"Why?" Marcella's arched brows snapped together. "The anger stage of grief?"

Sophie laughed, bitterly. "If only it were that." She blew out a breath and said it. "Sheldon Hamilton is Todd Remarkian, *and he's* the Ghost cyber vigilante. *And* he's very much still alive, after letting me believe he was dead." Everything around her felt too bright, and a buzzing noise filled her ears. She made herself blink.

"What?" Marcella wore a wine-colored dress that looked great with her bold coloring, but as she paled, the dress reminded Sophie of old blood against her sallow skin. "Say that again."

"Get in my car so we can talk." Sophie wrenched open the driver's side door of the Lexus.

Marcella ran around to the passenger side and got in as Sophie shut her door.

"You have to go grab Hamilton before he disappears." Sophie turned on the vehicle to activate the air conditioning.

"I can't, without probable cause!" Color flooded back into Marcella's cheeks. "What the hell is going on?"

"Here's what happened." Sophie outlined the events of the original case that had put her onto the Ghost's existence. "I didn't tell you, or Lei, or anyone—but I began a relationship with the Ghost online." She lowered her eyes. "I'm not proud of it. But he fascinated me."

"Go on." Marcella's voice was steely. She had taken her phone out, recording Sophie.

"I didn't know who he was, for sure, but I thought the Ghost was Sheldon Hamilton. I first got involved with him while trying to capture him, but later…I began to have feelings for him, and he led me to believe it was mutual. Later, when I started dating Todd but was going to reject him in favor of Sheldon, who was supposedly overseas…Todd revealed that Sheldon Hamilton was an alias of his."

Marcella's gaze was sharp and hard. "And you didn't tell me any of this."

"No. I was…caught up in his games, I guess. I thought what we had was *real*." She pushed a fist into her aching solar plexus, hunching over the pain. "Truth be known, I was intrigued by his version of justice. His whole purpose in life was his vigilantism. But he said he'd fallen in love with me, and had to be honest with me. And so, he shared his secret with me." Sophie raised her eyes to Marcella. "He even said he'd give up the vigilantism because I wasn't okay with it. And now you know how honest he really was with me. Now go arrest him, before he disappears again."

But Marcella's mouth had tightened and her eyes narrowed. *Sophie wasn't the only one feeling betrayed.* "Why didn't you tell me?"

"I just couldn't." Sophie opened her mouth and closed it, unable to find words, unable to say anything that would make her choice any more palatable to her friend. She looked down. "I'm sorry."

Without a word, Marcella jumped out of the car, slammed the door, and headed back toward the memorial service at a run.

Sophie didn't want to watch what happened next.

She had to get away. Clear her head. If she stayed around here, she'd be dragged into interviews, into testifying, into potentially seeing that man again. And the last thing she ever wanted to do was see or speak to the Ghost—*because whatever his real name was, the Ghost was all he was.*

Sophie put her foot on the accelerator and pulled out, headed for her father's apartment, breaking speed limits.

Chapter Thirty-Four

Frank Smithson frowned as Sophie threw her few clothes into her bag along with her satellite-compatible laptop. "Where are you going?"

Sophie glanced up at his weathered, handsome face.

"Dad." She walked over, embraced him, and leaned her head on his shoulder for a moment. He'd begun the retirement process from his ambassador job with a series of longer and longer leaves, using up his vacation time, and he'd been home during her latest crisis. "I'm sorry. The funeral was really upsetting. I need some time alone. I thought I'd go back to my apartment for a while."

He squeezed her close, his deep voice a comforting rumble. "I'm always glad to see my girl, even for a little while when she's stressed out."

"That was a nice way of describing my last couple of days lolling around depressed." Sophie had hardly anything personal left there, but she took an extra moment to check the drawers under the bed and the closet. "Thanks for taking care of Ginger."

"Always happy to spend time with my other girl." He played absently with the Lab's ears. "You taking her with you?"

"Of course." A plan was forming in her mind, but Sophie wasn't about to share it with her father at this point. "I'll be in touch as soon as I have a phone."

"Don't take too long about it. After recent events, we now have a three-day rule on being in touch."

"I hear you." Her father was tall enough that she had to go on tiptoes to kiss his cheek. "I'll get the phone today and text you. Talk soon."

She slipped on her backpack, tweaked Ginger's leash, and headed out.

———

MARY WATSON's apartment had been unoccupied long enough to develop a musty smell. Ginger nosed around and lapped thirstily when her bowl was freshened. Bright sunshine streamed in, and Sophie opened the sliders and windows, letting in a draft of plumeria scent from the big tree beside the building. She emptied her backpack in the bedroom, sorting her belongings from the stint on Maui, and organizing them to help identify what she would need for her plan.

Sitting down, Sophie made a careful list of supplies and errands. First, she needed to go to her bank.

After making sure Ginger had been fed, watered, and done her business on the patch of grass outside the run-down apartment building, Sophie headed out in Mary's truck.

She took the vehicle to a used car lot and haggled a deal, leaving the truck there and pocketing even less cash than the beat-up old vehicle was worth. At the bank, she accessed her safe deposit box, then pulled out all the money currently in her account, pocketing some cash from that transaction, and carrying out a cashier's check made out to the name of her third identity, Sandy Mason. At a second bank, she emptied Mary Watson's account and closed it, removing the cash from that as well. Outside, at a corner kiosk, she bought a reggae-themed trucker hat and a pair of cheap round sunglasses. She walked across the street to a third bank and opened a new account under the passport ID she'd removed from the safe deposit box in the name of Sandy Mason.

Sophie had learned the technique known as the "gray man" during her training at Quantico, with updated lessons from Connor. *The trick to moving around undetected was to blend.* She was a distinctive-looking woman, so effort had to be made to downplay her unique appearance. She'd created a recognizable but unremarkable persona as Mary Watson; she could do it again with Sandy Mason. Even new identity names had to be "gray"—common enough to be forgettable, but not so bland that they were an obvious alias.

Sophie went to a thrift store and bought an entire wardrobe for her new identity, a bohemian athlete, for under a hundred dollars. Finally, she went to a large sporting goods store and found the remaining items on her detailed list, paying for them in cash.

She took the clothing she'd just purchased to the laundromat. While the clothes were washing, she used the time to strip the tags and packaging off of all the outdoor gear she'd bought. Ignoring looks from other denizens of the laundromat, she unearthed a brand-new backpack with a lightweight carbon fiber frame and waist support strap.

When the clothing was clean and dry, she packed the bag, choosing only the items that would work in the environment she was headed for.

Sophie was pleased at how comfortable the gear was, how light the pack felt when she donned it wearing her new pair of waterproof hiking boots. *She'd never gone overnight backpacking before, and it was past time she tried a little outdoor living.* She walked, wearing the pack, to a nearby health food store.

By the time food was added to the pack, she was rethinking her initial assessment of the gear being light.

On the bus back to her apartment, Sophie worked on setting up a new phone, briefly accessing her contacts in the Cloud and loading them onto the new, satellite-capable smartphone she'd bought for Sandy Mason. She sent a text to her father from the number. She debated about her friends Marcella and Lei, and decided to wait to contact them.

Her finger hovered over Jake's name.

He'd been so good to her. A friend as much as a partner. She'd never forget how perfect it had been to lean on him at the fake memorial.

But he was always wanting more, and she had nothing to give. She was a liability as a friend. *And he wouldn't like what she was doing.*

She slid the phone into the pocket of the rip-stop camouflage cargo pants Sandy favored, and tugged on the bus's cable for her stop.

Back at the apartment, Sophie checked the airlines. Interisland flights with room for dogs were unregulated, and there was a plane out that afternoon. Holding the postcard with its photo of Kalalau, she considered. She really should wait until she knew whether or not she was being charged with Assan's murder.

But if she was charged, she'd be stuck here on Oahu.

Stuck in Sophie Ang's life. Going through a trial. Maybe even to jail. Truth was, she wasn't willing to go to jail for Assan, no matter what she was charged with.

Sophie Ang's future looked bleak. It was time for a change, on a number of levels.

If the Ghost could pull off a total identity change, so could Sandy Mason. The only person who really needed to know that she was alive was her father, and she would send him a text every three days without letting him know where she was. She stuck the postcard behind a magnet on the fridge, made reservations, and secured a kennel on the flight for Ginger.

Today was the day she left behind half measures and stepped into a new life entirely.

Sophie left Ginger in the apartment and headed down to the landlord's office. The man's greasy pate gleamed in an overhead light as he opened the door of his unit. "What you like, sistah?" He scratched a basketball-sized belly, sausaged into a University of Hawaii jersey.

"Paying for six months in advance." All of Mary's transactions with him had been in cash, so this was nothing unusual. She handed him a stack of money. "I will be coming and going as I have been."

"Why you gone so much?" The little Portuguese man's beady eyes assessed her from behind thick glasses.

"I travel for work." Sophie handed him another hundred. "And I like my privacy. In case anyone comes here asking for me, I don't live here anymore."

"Then I need a little something more for security." The man kept his hand out, and she put several more hundreds in it. He tucked the cash into his pocket. "Safe journeys, then, sistah." A gold tooth gleamed in his grin, and he closed the door.

It was easy to disappear in a neighborhood like this. She should have let the apartment go, but knowing she had somewhere to return to helped her detach.

Sophie headed back upstairs and unlocked the apartment door.

Ginger gave a *woof* from inside, but didn't come out to greet her. When she opened the door, she saw why.

Chapter Thirty-Five

S heldon Hamilton sat in one of her kitchen chairs, rubbing Ginger's ears. He took off the white straw hat and set it on the table, revealing short-cropped dark hair. "She remembers me."

The dog panted happily, her tongue lolling in a grin as the man stroked her. Sophie's skin twitched, remembering how good it felt to be touched by him.

"I remember you too, *Connor*. If that's really your name." Sophie kept her face and voice neutral with difficulty as anger rose in a blistering wave. Looking at him, she distinctly remembered the strenuous and satisfying sensation of cutting Assan's throat. She eyed the Ghost. *She could take him.* Her knife was gone, taken into evidence, but she had other means.

"I regret how this unfolded. I brought flowers." The man leaned aside so she could see a large, perfectly round topiary made of fresh, dark red rosebuds blooming up from a green velvet box. *Trust him to bring something unique and special.*

"Flowers." Sophie turned and shut the door, locking it automatically. "Going to take a little more than that to apologize for letting me grieve your death." She refused to make eye contact, looking at a spot to the left of his shoulder.

"I know." He remained seated. "I had reasons. And I'm sorry."

"Reasons. That I can believe." Sophie walked into the kitchen and set down her purse. She glanced at the closed door of the bedroom, glad she'd left the backpack inside as she filled a water glass, ignoring him as she sipped. *She didn't want him to know what she was planning.*

But he'd broken in, and her phone alarm had not gone off. He'd likely searched the apartment. Might even have it bugged.

The best strategy was to confront him and get it over with. *But she didn't want to, and that was the honest truth.* She'd run away to avoid ever having to look into his artificially brown eyes again. Maybe telling him that was the place to start.

Sophie squared her shoulders and walked back to the Ghost. "I don't want to have this conversation. I left the memorial because I never wanted to see you again."

"And I just got out of a very uncomfortable interview with the FBI that I never wanted to have," he said mildly.

"Good." Anger, the fuel she needed, wafted up her body to tighten her fists. "It was past time I shared what I knew about the Ghost."

"And I expected you to. Which is why I let you think I was dead. I needed time to solidify Sheldon's identity. Todd's murder wasn't on my timetable. Todd was killed by your ex, in case you were wondering. Actually, someone hired by your ex. I was able to track the bomber."

They locked gazes for a long moment. Sophie hated the way his eyes looked with the contact lenses in. She sank into a chair at the table opposite him. "You talk about Todd as if he were real."

"Todd had begun to feel real to me." The man took off the glasses. Reached into his pocket and retrieved a contact lens case. With a couple of economical gestures, he removed the brown lenses, and Connor's familiar sea-blue eyes looked at her. He reached across the table for her hand.

She jerked away. "Connor. Is your name Connor? I don't know what to call you any more now that I found out Todd's middle name is Colin."

"My real name is Connor. I told you the truth about that. I told you the truth about a lot of it. Just not everything. Because I wasn't sure you wouldn't turn me in."

"And I didn't. Until this morning."

"Right." He blew out a breath, ran a hand through his dark hair. The sight of his familiar hands still did things to her insides that she now wanted to forget. "I came home from Maui and our time together." He looked up and held her gaze. Images of them in bed at the hostel in Paia filled her memory. "While we were there, I had detected an infiltration into my Pendragon Arches apartment via my surveillance app, but chose to ignore it in favor of being with you and dealing with it when I got back. I'm not sorry for that decision."

Sophie looked away. "You could have told me about that."

"But I didn't. You had enough on your mind. Once back on Oahu, outside my apartment, I was concerned that the apartment's surveillance AI, whose cameras had been neutralized, registered the presence of explosives." Connor stood at last. He paced, tension and fatigue in the slump of his shoulders. "The apartment was wired to blow, and it occurred to me that this was a good time to get out." Ginger got up and walked back and forth with him, inserting her head beneath his hand, and he petted her absently. "The FBI was closing in on the Ghost. Though the investigation into the dead agent was planted, they had begun to put together other cases that were attributable to the Ghost. Your friend, Ken Yamada, had what you both found on that first case and they were digging deeper into Todd, into Security Solutions. And I had an exit strategy planned for Todd's identity, should I ever need it."

"Don't tell me. A cadaver that looked like Todd with dental records doctored to match," Sophie said, unable to keep the bitterness out of her voice. "You deserve to be caught. You ran from an investigation. You let me believe you had died!" She bit her lip. "*Foul tumor on the devil's backside!* Do you have any idea what it was like to pour over your body in the morgue, trying to identify you? Wondering, all the while, if you could possibly have been devious enough to set the whole thing up?"

"I imagine it was…unpleasant."

"Your toes, Connor." Sophie met his gaze with her hard one. "The only unique thing about your body. How handy that they were gone. And no DNA on file or in your apartment? Masterful. But I bet Sheldon Hamilton has DNA in abundance and on record."

"He does. I put a lot of effort and planning into these identities." Connor paused in his pacing, his hands on his hips. If possible, the brown hair and darkened brows, contrasting with his light eyes, made him more handsome.

She wanted to hate the sight of him. "And I bet you have a cadaver somewhere that matches Sheldon Hamilton."

He didn't reply to that. "Do you want to know how I dealt with the bomb?"

"Not particularly."

"Nevertheless." Connor walked to the sink, poured himself a glass of water, and returned to sit. He sipped. "I went into the "Batcave" and used the surveillance equipment in that unit to identify the whereabouts of the bomb. I was able to pause the mechanism, which was motion activated but with a timer. I retrieved the body from its storage location and placed it near the bomb. I removed all of the DNA trace I could find in the place. And then I activated the explosion."

"Why couldn't you have told me you were alive in the note you left me at the bank?" Sophie's question was a cry from the heart. "I held onto hope until then!"

"I wanted to let you go. And I wanted you to let *me* go. I'm bad for you." His eyes were wide and stark, pleading for her to understand. "After I left you in Paia, I realized I never should have said I would give up my brand of justice, my mission. It would compromise my very self to do so. I'd have to tell you that, and you'd likely break up with me. This seemed like...a good solution. You would grieve and move on. I would learn to live without you, somewhere else in the world, and I'd continue my work as Sheldon Hamilton."

"So why did you come back to your memorial then?" Sophie's lips felt numb. The words seemed to come from somewhere else. "No one would have caught on to Sheldon Hamilton abroad."

"I couldn't stay away." He whispered. "I missed you too much. I hurt, seeing how badly I had hurt you."

"I don't...I can't." Sophie stood. "I want you to leave." She pointed at the door.

"We can still make this work." He stood, but slowly, as if his joints hurt. "Sheldon may be on a watch list, but they will never be able to prove I'm Todd Remarkian."

"Unless they catch you with your contacts off." Sophie shook her head. "No. I grieved you. Grieved the love we had. I won't live a lie. I won't pretend you aren't who I know you are, doing what I know you are doing. I can't."

"So, you're off to live your own lie." His eyes gleamed turquoise.

Sophie winced at the accuracy. *He'd seen the backpack.* Likely watched her every move since she left the funeral. She needed to check her belongings thoroughly for tracking devices.

"Maybe so. But I prefer to think of this next chapter as finding myself, and I'm not hurting anyone while I do it."

"Except for the minor detail of killing your ex and a possible murder charge."

"Some people just need killing, and well you know it."

"Hypocrite."

"Liar. Murderer." She pointed at the door. "Now go."

"Give me the Ghost software."

That square lump of metal and silicate was weighing down the bottom of her backpack, and she wasn't about to give it back to him. "No."

"I thought you'd want to be rid of it."

"I'm not going to help you do your dirty work."

"Fine. I have another copy, of course. And I trust you'll see the bigger picture enough at least to keep the software out of anyone else's hands. Including law enforcement."

Sophie folded her lips shut and her arms over her chest, refusing to answer. She had no idea what she was going to do with the Ghost software, only that she wasn't giving it back to him.

Connor took a step toward her. "I love you." He opened his hands in a surrender gesture. "Let's figure this out."

Sophie didn't move. "I believe that you love me as much as you will ever love anyone. But I will never trust you again, and that's no basis for a relationship. Please go. Before I'm forced to call the FBI and tell them you're here."

"I won't give up on you, whether you want me to or not. You can always contact me at that chatroom we first used."

"I won't call you." Sophie felt strong, determined, and numb. "I'm going off the grid and you won't be able to find me."

"I can always find you," he said calmly. She did not reply. Connor headed to the bathroom. "I need a moment."

He put the contacts back into his eyes at the sink. She slid her phone out of her pocket, considering whether or not to video him doing so. She decided not to. *That was forgiveness.*

Connor washed his hands, blinking at her with newly darkened eyes. She stared back expressionlessly.

He turned and gave Ginger one last pat. "Thanks for looking after Anubis."

"I love that dog. And I loved you. Don't ever approach me again."

Connor nodded, once. "I hope you'll forgive me. Someday." He slipped out the door.

Chapter Thirty-Six

K alalau Valley, on Kaua'i, was a rugged twelve-mile hike along precipitous cliffs from its starting point, and almost impossible to do in one day. Sophie planned to take it in stages, hiking as far as Sandy and her dog, Gracie, felt like, then camping. *After all, they weren't in a hurry.* This was the first day of their new lives, and having cut all ties, Sophie wanted to savor that freedom.

Sandy Mason hadn't bothered with a rental car, instead opting for a ride-sharing lift from the airport to Ke'e Beach, a stunning half-moon cove at the base of the velvety-green Na Pali Coast, an area so rugged it was completely untamed by roads.

Sophie hoped she fooled the facial recognition at the airports by wearing the reggae-themed hat to duck cameras and using colorful face paint with white peace symbols on her cheeks, as if making a political statement, to confuse the software. While she'd gotten some stares, Sandy Mason was a proud pacifist.

"Disguise is sleight of hand," Connor had told her once. "You say, 'Look here!' while really, you go there." Sophie wiped off the paint once outside the airport but kept on the hat and the round sunglasses. She wore light but sturdy hiking pants, boots, and a sleeveless shirt with a marijuana leaf on the front.

Mary Watson and Sophie Ang were gone, but Sandy Mason blended well with the locals on Kaua'i at first glance. Sophie hoped that the Sandy identity struck that perfect balance between bland and forgettable—though Ginger-Gracie made anonymity challenging. The Lab's friendliness and sweet nature were a human lure.

Gracie was a weakness that couldn't be helped. Sophie'd given up everything. She couldn't lose her dog, too.

Sophie looked up a slanting trail studded with large boulders. Huge java plum and mango trees, cascading with tropical vines, hung down to touch shoulders of a red-dirt trail clothed in bamboo grass. Guava trees dripped bright yellow fruit like Easter eggs among the ferns. Her heart sped up with anticipation.

After a final pit stop to use the restroom and fill up a heavy water jug, Sophie walked past the sign-in book in the kiosk at the base of the trail without logging in. She hefted the pack and buckled it on. Ignoring the *No Dogs Allowed* sign, she tweaked Ginger's leash and set off up the trail.

After so much emotion and mental anguish, it felt great to simply pit herself against a physical challenge. Even with care in organizing her supplies, the backpack still weighed more than fifty pounds, and the trail was steep, rutted, and studded with rocks that required concentration.

Sophie's favorite pastime of run-hiking on Oahu stood her in good stead, though, and she pushed upward, picking up a sturdy bamboo staff a returning hiker had left leaning against a tree.

Exiting the jungle at the first hairpin turn of the cliffs, Sophie dropped her stick and gasped at the glorious sight of the staggered row of crenellated cliffs marching down the Na Pali Coast all the way to Kalalau.

Waves crashed against the black lava cliffs far below, aqua in shallow areas, cobalt as the water got deeper. Sophie gazed into a horizon lacy with spume from the brisk wind that dried the sweat on her cheeks and body. She reached into the pocket of her cargo pants and pulled out a postcard of these very breathtaking cliffs that she'd bought in the airport. She held it up, comparing. *Yes, the photo had been taken from this spot.*

The view before her was even better than the picture on the postcard that Connor had left pinned on her side of the "Batcave." *She had him to thank for the inspiration for this trip.*

And now it was time for goodbye.

Sophie reached into her pocket again and took out a small baggie containing the torn-up scraps of the note Connor had left her in the safe deposit box, the note pledging his love. *Love he meant, in his way.* That was why it hurt to dump the scraps into her palm and toss them off the cliff and into the void.

Wind swirled up and caught the tiny white snowflake bits, whirling them into the sky above Sophie's head for a brief moment, before sweeping them out to sea.

Sophie wished she could dig into the backpack and pick up the brick of the Ghost software and throw it off the cliff, too. *Even though he lived, that program had taken him from her.*

But she wasn't quite ready to do that. Maybe there was still some redemptive possibility for the software when she cracked it and mastered it. But that would wait for another day. Today was full of new beginnings and possibility.

A pure-white tropicbird with a forked tail dove like a kite above the black cliffs, making her smile. Far off in the distance over the ocean, a towering cumulus cloud trailed a rainsquall lit with a rainbow. And right in front of her, the red-dirt trail beckoned.

Sophie had paid a high price for a whole new life to step into and explore, and now it was time to begin.

"Come on, Gracie. Let's go," Sandy Mason said, and picked up her bamboo walking stick.

Acknowledgments

Aloha dear readers!

You know the old saying: things are always darkest before the dawn?

Yeah, that. But I like to think a white tropicbird off the Na Pali Coast and a cloud trailing a rainbow are signs that things will be brighter in *Wired Dawn*! I personally have witnessed these visual miracles off the Na Pali Coast, and they are too good not to share.

Sophie has had to go dark, and deep, wrestling with the issues of love, conscience, justice, and identity that are her particular challenge. Will she have a happy ending? I don't know; she hasn't told me yet. She's still growing and changing, and so are the various men who've fallen in love with her. You'll just have to read on and see! But I have to say, not knowing who she will settle on from the various awesome choices is pretty darn fun!

I want to thank some folks: Don and Bonnie, reader fans who have become friends and my copyeditors for this series. They have done a great job keeping track of timelines, dangler clues, repeat words, and my penchant for "accidentally" using known or recycled names for characters—for instance, I had Shank Miller have the real name of Steve Miller, and apparently, there's a well-known rocker by that name. Duh. I knew that. On some level.

Don and Bonnie are wine aficionados, and this year flew out to join me at my temporary residence in Sonoma County wine country (long story, family situation) and we got to go wine tasting and get to know each other in real life.

I also want to thank my faithful and amazing proofreaders Shirley LaCroix, Angie Lail, and Bonnie Thompson. These eagle-eyed ladies try to catch everything that Don, Bonnie and I miss. Mahalos forever for being on my team!

I love how my writing has brought me friends that feel like family from all over the world, and I'm so glad you are a part of that "ohana" too, by joining Sophie's (and Lei's!) journeys.

I'm super excited about Sophie's next phase; the mystery we have to solve is ripped straight out of the headlines: there's a group of people living in the back of Kalalau Valley on Kaua'i, and strange things are happening! So be sure to read on to the excerpt from *Wired Dawn*, book 5 in the Paradise Crime Series.

As always, if you enjoyed this book, please leave a review! You have no idea how much they mean to an author, and to a book's success. Mahalo nui loa, as we say in Hawaii!

I hope you'll continue Sophie's story with *Wired Dawn*, and join me on any or all of the social media outlets (listed at the end) where I love to get to know readers, beginning with my Facebook group, Friends of Toby Neal Books.

Read on for an excerpt from *Wired Dawn*, and until next time, I'll be writing!

Much aloha,

Toby Neal

———

I hope you enjoyed *Wired Dark*. If you think other readers will enjoy it too, please leave an honest review on Amazon, Barnes & Noble, Goodreads, iBooks, or Kobo. Your thoughts matter so much, and I read them all!

Want two FREE full length, award-winning books from Toby Neal? *Visit* www.subscribepage.com/TobyNealNews
Love romance thrillers? Check out Toby Neal & Emily Kimelman's hot new apocalyptic *Scorch Series at* http://tobyandemily.pagedemo.co/

Read on for a sample of the next book in the series!

Excerpt | Wired Dawn

Chapter 1

The boy ran, stumbling in the darkness, toward the farthest black corner of the cave. His breath tore through his lungs with a sound like ripping fabric as he put his hands out, slowing as the fire got further away and the darkness thickened, its flickering light dimming. He tripped and almost fell on the loose, jagged stones of the cavern floor.

That voice like warm honey that he'd once listened to called his name. "Come, Nakai. What you running for?"

Nakai reached the back corner of the cave, a dark and drafty spot where he could feel fresh air welling like spring water from somewhere deep in the earth.

The man's footsteps were coming—smooth, unhurried, confident. Nakai glanced back and saw the flashlight swinging, illuminating the harsh, volcanic stone walls with every swing. "Stop this foolishness, boy."

Frantic, Nakai felt down the wall to the vent, finding a small cleft. He wriggled through.

The pitch darkness on the other side of the wall was thick as a muffling black blanket. Nakai crawled forward on his hands and knees, biting his lips to keep from whimpering at the pain of rocks digging into his hands and knees.

"What, boy? You trying fo' get away?" The voice was a sibilant hiss, the sound of evil disguised as a friend, the sound of the worst kind of betrayal. Even now, the boy's skin crawled at the memory of the man's hands on him, touching him, stroking and petting, pinching and forcing. "You want to leave so bad? You go then. And sleep well in the dark."

Nakai stopped, holding his breath, turning back toward the slit illuminated by the flashlight's beam. He heard the scrape of a rock, and then the light blinked out.

He was in total darkness, and he was trapped.

Nakai turned around and felt his way back in the direction from which he'd come.

Panic rose in a strangling wave and sweat burst out over his body as he crawled forward, and forward, and forward—and felt nothing ahead. No cleft, no wall.

He was lost in the dark already.

"Let me out! Help me!"

The stone seemed to vibrate around him, as if he sat in the middle of a giant drum. "That's why music sounds so good in the cave," the man had told the circle of boys on Nakai's first night with the group of runaways he called the Lost Boys. "This lava tube goes on for miles, and the porousness of the stone makes sound carry."

Maybe it would carry his calls for help. "Let me out!" Nakai cried again. "Help! I'm stuck in here!"

Nothing but the faintest echo of his terror came back to him.

Nakai crawled rapidly now, heedless of bleeding hands and knees, determined to at least hit some kind of wall ahead—but suddenly, he was out in space and falling into blackness that swallowed his scream.

———

Special Agent Marcella Scott stood on a battered rubber mat outside the door of a shitty apartment on a run-down street in a bad part of Honolulu. The gritty zone of heat-shimmering concrete block buildings was sandwiched between the airport and a military installation, and the discordant sound of traffic going by on a nearby overpass competed with the wail of a police siren. The only thing that showed that the apartment was even in Hawaii was a battered and dusty plumeria tree on one side of the building. Its fragrant pinwheel blossoms sent up a waft of sweet scent, and Marcella closed her eyes and breathed it in, then reached out and knocked.

No one answered.

She wasn't surprised. She knocked again.

No answer.

Marcella dug in her pocket and brought out a thick bunch of keys. Her fiancé, Marcus, always told her to thin them out. "You could do yourself an injury with that wad of keys," he teased. "Throw your back out carrying them, or at least bruise your ass sitting with them in your back pocket."

Marcella laughed, but didn't thin out the thick ring with its plastic New Jersey souvenir tag. *A girl had to remember where she was from.* And Marcella loved keys. A key meant you were trusted, had access, and could get in.

And she was the only person besides the occupant to have access to this particular door.

She flipped through the thick ring: home, FBI office, parents' apartment, car, post office box, and on and on until she came to a brass Schlage. Two, actually, connected on a little ring —because just one wasn't enough for security-conscious Sophie Ang.

Sophie.

Her friend had dealt her a blow of betrayal that still had

Marcella's temper flaring hot under her tidily buttoned blouse if she thought about it too long.

And Sophie was likely holed up in the apartment, the blackout drapes drawn, deep in one of her depression cycles. Angry as Marcella was with her friend, Sophie needed her.

Marcella opened the thumb lock and with the other key, the deadbolt, pushing the door inward. "Sophie?"

She felt the emptiness of the place instantly.

No Ginger, Sophie's energetic yellow Lab, running to greet her. The place smelled stale and sour, but she called again, anyway. "Soph!"

No answer.

She shut and locked the door. Sophie wasn't at her father's; Frank Smithson had been the one to call Marcella to go check on his daughter. "She has a three-day window to contact me, and it's been four days. You know how she gets, and where she hides," he'd asked her this morning. "Can you go by her place?"

This bolt hole of Sophie's was rented in the name of her alias, Mary Watson, and Marcella was literally the only one who knew where it was.

She wrinkled her nose at the smell of garbage that had been left under the sink. She opened the refrigerator. Very little inside. She walked into the back bedroom. The bed Marcella and Frank had bought for Sophie was neatly made up—but the sense of emptiness persisted.

Marcella opened the closet and frowned. The hangers were empty.

She opened the drawers of the dresser. Nothing inside.

Sophie was gone.

Marcella straightened, heart rate spiking. She hurried now, whipping open the drawers of the desk. Everything was removed but a notepad and some leftover office detritus: a few Post-its and pens, some tape. The monitor Sophie plugged into her high-end laptop when she was here was still there, but every personal anything that belonged to her friend was gone.

Would Sophie have run? Did she not trust the system that much? And what would happen if that grandstanding DA decided to go ahead with a murder rap? It would be wrong, but the jerk might be trying to garner headlines in the courtroom. *You never knew these days…*

Marcella heard the sound of a key in the front door lock. She raced back into the front room, whipping the door open.

"Sophie!" Her friend's name died on Marcella's lips at the sight of a short man with a greasy comb over and a belly straining a football jersey that had seen better days.

Brown eyes blinked at her from behind thick glasses. "Eh, sistah. Whatchu doing heah?"

Marcella's hand had fallen automatically to her weapon. "FBI. Who the hell are you?"

The man's eyes widened and he took a step back. "Building manager. I nevah know notting what dis renter was doing in heah."

Marcella held her cred wallet up for the man to see. "I need to know where she is."

The manager's gaze darted up to the left. *He was considering what to tell her, how much to lie.*

Marcella softened her voice and stance. "Sorry if I gave the wrong impression. The woman who lives here is missing and I'm looking for her. She didn't do anything wrong." *At least I hope not.*

"I nevah know notting," the manager repeated.

Marcella shot out a hand and grabbed him by the wrist, yanking the man inside the apartment. He stumbled across the threshold with a little yelp and she slammed the door. "Where is she? Tell me now, or I'll take you in for questioning."

"She paid me for six months in advance!" the manager burst out. "She said no tell anyone she lived here anymore. Said she was going to be in and out. Nevah said notting about no FBI!"

Marcella looked him over. Sweat had popped out in beads on his brow and upper lip. His gaze darted around the room.

He was telling the truth.

"Did she tell you where she was going?"

"No. Only that she liked her privacy."

So, Sophie had anticipated Marcella would come looking and paid this jerk to keep quiet about it. Anger rose in a hot flash.

"Get out of here," Marcella snapped. "And you better not rent this place out from under her. But if you see her, tell her the FBI is looking for her."

The man scrambled to the door and slammed it shut behind him.

Marcella took several deep breaths, trying to calm herself. *That bitch!* Some friend Sophie was, first holding back intel about the Ghost, next pulling a disappearing act when she might be facing a murder charge!

Marcella's eyes landed on a colorful postcard held onto the rusting, avocado-colored fridge with a magnet.

She walked over and removed a scene of the stunning Na Pali Cliffs, their corrugated, jutting green expanse marching into a blue horizon like an endless row of green, Chinese clay soldiers. A caption in yellow at the bottom blared, *Visit Kalalau, Kaua'i!*

Marcella slipped the card into her pocket. She wrinkled her nose at the smell of the garbage.

Who knew when Sophie would be back? It would be awful to come home to this reek.

Marcella pulled the white trash can liner out of the plastic can, tying it tight, and looked around one last time. "I'm going to find you, Sophie," she muttered. "You can run, but you can't hide."

―――――

Sophie folded her damp tent as tightly as she could, but still, somehow, the damn thing had expanded. She usually had to refold it several times before she could get it back into the bag, and the ever-present, bright red Kauaʻi mud adhering to the slick plastic bottom made her hands and knees filthy.

"No one told me how dirty you get camping," she remarked to Ginger. The Lab looked on, tongue lolling in her usual doggy grin. Sophie had taken to talking to Ginger as days went by without other human contact.

There had been other hikers on the trail to Kalalau, of course. She and Ginger had done the rugged twelve-mile hike in three segments as she got used to carrying the heavy pack and working her camp stove, water filtration system, assembling and breaking down her tent and gear. She'd sent her obligatory text on the third day to her father, letting him know she was still alive, but her phone told her No Signal.

"That Lyft driver said it was ambitious to take on Kalalau as a first-time backpacker," Sophie said, scrunching the tent down tightly. "I think he might have been right." Ginger woofed in agreement. The Lab's coat was rough with mud; it had rained off and on for the five days they'd been out here. "Maybe it will be drier deeper inside the valley if we can find a ridge."

Finally wrestling the filthy tent into its zip-up container, Sophie finished breaking camp, brushing leaves and soil over her fire ring. She'd camped near the stream and hadn't seen a soul since she finally arrived at the remote place, with its famously stunning, jungle-clothed valley arms that opened from a peak in Kokee and spread into a wide, lush valley that ended at a massive beach and the wide blue sea.

But the beach was populated with other campers and frequented daily by boatloads of tourists who came by Zodiac from Port Allen on the south coast, sunburnt and loud, their juice boxes and sandwiches and snorkel gear celebrating a vacation in paradise…and Sophie wasn't here for a vacation.

She wasn't entirely sure *why* she was here, except that she had needed to get away and start a new life, and the postcard that had led her here had drawn her, with its gorgeous capture of the extreme beauty of this setting.

She'd fled Oahu and her life there. Fled a broken heart, a possible murder charge, even her own pattern of falling into a black hole of depression.

So far, the crazy idea had worked to keep her demons at bay. Hiking and learning to survive out here had been a total distraction: she was too tired by nightfall to wonder or worry, happy to burrow into her tiny tent with her dog, and sleep the deep and uncomplicated sleep of the physically exhausted.

The depression medication might be working, too. For the first time in her life she'd resorted to that, but the circumstances had dictated radical intervention. She had a three-month supply, and hopefully she'd be ready to resume a normal life by the time her prescription ran out.

Or maybe not. But she didn't have to know right now.

Sophie popped the little white pill into her mouth and swished it back with a mouthful of water she'd filtered and boiled from the nearby stream. "Come, girl. Let's go."

Ginger fell in next to Sophie as she pushed ahead in wet-dry hiking shoes onto a narrow trail, slick with iron-rich red mud, winding between tall banks of pili grass and wild guava trees. The smell of wet grass, mold, and the sweetness of rotting guavas flavored the air. Sophie plucked a yellow guava off one of the trees and bit into it as she pushed forward, already feeling the forty-pound pack's weight sinking heavily onto her hips. She paused to tighten the belt so the weight didn't land on her lower back.

She took another bite of the firm, tangy guava, enjoying the sweet-sour pink flesh as she paused to look around at the soaring, green-robed sides of the valley. This place reminded her of Waipio Valley on the Big Island, her first real exposure to this environment—and a case that had scarred her for life.

She shut down the memory of that place, that case—and her partner Jake, who'd saved her life.

Jake.

She wouldn't think of him, of her conflicted feelings about

and toward him. Because that reminded her of Connor. And Connor didn't deserve anything from her, at all.

Sophie pushed forward faster, bumping into Ginger and urging the dog into a trot. She used the sturdy bamboo stick she'd picked up on the first day she left to push branches out of the way and for leverage as she hiked as rapidly as physically able straight toward the back of the valley.

She'd heard from some other hikers that there was some kind of settlement back there, renegade local people who refused to honor the five-day permits issued by the state for camping. She was ignoring the five-day limit too, and thus needed to avoid the areas patrolled by state park rangers.

The trail meandered along the clear stream, climbing steadily back toward the steep head of the valley where the junction of the valley walls boasted a waterfall that plummeted hundreds of feet.

Sophie paused eventually to let Ginger drink from the stream and to drink herself, from a canteen of boiled water. At each elevation, she paused to look back at the view down toward the ocean, to savor a slight breeze that dried sweat brought to the surface of her skin by effort and humidity.

She wanted to see that waterfall, and then she'd pick another campsite, one with enough openness that hopefully she'd get her gear dried out, and be able to connect her satellite-ready laptop with some wireless internet.

She hadn't been online for five days, an eternity for someone as "wired in" as she normally was. After the first couple of days of free-floating anxiety, she'd come to enjoy the anonymous feeling of being unplugged.

She was well and truly off the grid.

Finally.

And she'd left everything and everyone behind to go—including her name and identity. Her father. Her friends Lei and Marcella.

It was all the Ghost's fault. *That bastard.* He'd let her grieve for him…

She shook her head to rid it of those buzzing, painful thoughts as she reached a small knoll surrounded with the bright yellow-green of kukui nut trees in full leaf. The remains of lo'i, the ancient Hawaiian terraces used in the cultivation of taro, provided a stacked rock wall that would block the wind. If she was under the trees, her camp would be out of the sun…*but she didn't want to be in sight of the path.*

"Come, Ginger." She turned off the trail and bushwhacked through waist-high ferns and undergrowth deep into the grove of kukui trees.

Looking up into their interlaced branches, she enjoyed the hum of the wind blowing across the trees. "This seems like a good spot."

She had just unslung her heavy pack, lowering it to the ground, when she heard the sound of gut-wrenching weeping, and a woman burst through the bushes, making Ginger sit up and bark.

"Help me! My son is gone!"

———

More Titles from Toby Neal!

Lei Crime Series
Paradise Crime Series
Michaels Family Romances
Scorch Series Romance Thrillers
Young Adult Novels

Visit TobyNeal.Net Today!

About the Author

Kirkus Reviews calls Neal's writing, "persistently riveting. Masterly."

 Award-winning, USA Today bestselling social worker turned author Toby Neal grew up on the island of Kaua`i in Hawaii. Neal is a mental health therapist, a career that has informed the depth and complexity of the characters in her stories. Neal's police procedurals, starring multicultural detective Lei Texeira, explore the crimes and issues of Hawaii from the bottom of the ocean to the top of volcanoes, and are so popular that they've spawned a licensed fan fiction world on Amazon. Fans call her stories, "Immersive, addicting, and the next best thing to being there."

You can connect with Toby on BookBub, Facebook, Goodreads, Google+, Instagram, Pinterest, and Twitter.

CPSIA information can be obtained
at www.ICGtesting.com
Printed in the USA
FSOW01n2300141117
41189FS